Open Your Heart
A Sensual Collection

Ali Spooner

Open Your Heart
A Sensual Collection

Ali Spooner

Affinity
eBook Press
NZ
2016

Open Your Heart
A Sensual Collection
© 2016 by Ali Spooner

Affinity E-Book Press NZ LTD
Canterbury, New Zealand

1st Edition

ISBN: 978-0-947528-36-2

Editor: Angela Koenig
Proof Editor: Alexis Smith
Cover Design: Irish Dragon Designs

Acknowledgments

I would like to thank my fans for following my stories, providing great feedback and encouragement. Writing wouldn't be so much fun without you.

Thanks to Affinity, for their patient editing, Irish Dragon for the cover art and the team of readers, who give me the gentle nudges to help me grow as a writer.

A special thanks to Suzy, who knows just when I need a kick in the pants to get me writing. Thanks my friends, you've been a tremendous support through some challenging times.

Dedication

To my partner Rhonda, and the brave souls who continue their fight against cancer.

Table of Contents

Open Your Heart   1
The Dreamer   32
The Perfect Gift   37
The Window Seat   72
The Dance   93
Hips, Lips, and Fingertips   100
Landfall   109
Consumed   131
Shooting Stars   157
All In   163
A Taste of Heaven   200
Three for the Show   203
About the Author   214
Other Books from Affinity eBook Press   215

Also by Ali Spooner

Single Stories

South of Heaven
Shotgun Rider
The Settlement
Love's Playlist
Cowgirl Up
Twisted Lives
The Epitaph
Terminal Event
Bailey's Run

Series

The Island Series
Neptune's Ring
Venus Rising

The Hunter Series
Bound
The Devil's Tree

Sasha Thibodaux Series
Sugarland
Bayou Justice
Line of Sight

Open Your Heart

"Don't look now, Hayden, but your stalker just arrived," Tory said.

Hayden turned on her bar stool and looked toward the entrance to the bar.

"I said don't look, you goof."

Two women were entering the bar. Hayden turned back and took a deep drink of her cocktail. "I would have thought she would have gotten tired of her game by now."

Tory chuckled and elbowed her companion. "Not until she gets a piece of you, my friend."

Hayden jerked her head around, her dark eyes glaring at Tory. "That will never happen. One time falling for a straight girl was enough for me."

Tory blanched at the vehemence in Hayden's words. She had almost forgotten Lauren, the woman who had quickly charmed Hayden into her bed, just to make a video on a dare from her boyfriend. Hayden had almost gone off the deep end, nearly drowning herself in depression when she found out how badly Lauren had screwed her over. The most disturbing fact was that she was genuinely attracted to

Lauren. Since then, the normally fun loving Hayden had become hard and distrustful of people she did not know well.

Tory watched as the two women sat at the same booth they had occupied for the past three weeks. She had to admit they were very attractive women, and one of them couldn't keep her eyes off of Hayden. She chuckled softly to herself. Hayden was one of the reasons that the bar packed full of women on a Friday night. Her dark Latino features were stunning and her moves on the dance floor went beyond erotic. Some nights when she was in 'a mood' people would stop on the dance floor just to watch her as she danced with a partner. She never lacked for a willing partner, and on many nights, she left the bar with the woman of her choice clinging tightly to her on the back of her BMW motorbike.

"If you weren't such a sexy beast, you wouldn't have every woman in the place chasing you," Tory said.

"You are so full of shit."

"That is one of the things I love about you, my friend. You have no clue just how gorgeous you are."

"You better order another drink, Tory. I think your vision is starting to fade."

Tory was about to do just that when Deana, the bartender, walked over and sat a fresh crown and coke in front of Hayden. "From your admirer," she said with a sweet smile.

"Thanks, Deana."

"Enjoy," Deana said, before turning around to return to filling orders.

Tory didn't even have a chance to order a fresh drink for herself before Deana was gone. "See, that is exactly what I mean."

"What are you talking about now?"

"I am sitting here, empty glass in front of me, and Deana brings you a fresh drink and doesn't even glance my way." With a deep laugh, Tory got up from the stool to walk over to where Deana was making drinks.

Hayden shook her head. She and Tory had been best friends for several years and she trusted no one like she did her. She felt lucky she had one true friend who, no matter what the circumstance, would always give her an honest opinion, even when she didn't ask for one. She knew though that Tory watched over her carefully and would have her back in any given situation.

Hayden reached over for the fresh drink and swirled the straw in the caramel colored liquid. If the straight girl wanted to play romantic and send her drinks, she would not refuse them, but it would be money unwisely spent if she thought she could buy Hayden's attentions. As she lifted the glass, she turned on her stool and nodded in appreciation to the woman who had sent the drink. She lifted the drink to her lips and took a sip, the cool liquid burning as she swallowed.

Tory returned to the stool beside Hayden. "Your favorite dance partner is on her way to ask you to dance."

"Julie is here?"

"Julie is right behind you, darling, and so needs to dance with you." Hayden heard the soft, sensual voice from behind them say.

Hayden turned and smiled at the petite woman standing in front of her. "I have missed you. Where have you been?"

"Reagan and I went on a short cruise."

"I am so glad you are back."

"Thanks. So get your cute ass out on the dance floor with me." Julie grabbed Hayden's hand and pulled her off the barstool.

Tory spun around to watch her friends on the dance floor. She glanced over at the booth and as expected, the woman who had her sights set on Hayden was transfixed as she watched Hayden and Julie on the dance floor. Tory saw the woman's friend say something and lean across the table when the woman did not respond.

Tory sipped on her drink and hummed, "Another one bites the dust."

On the dance floor, Hayden and Julie moved in one fluid motion. Julie turned around, falling into Hayden's arms confident that she would gently catch her and pull her close.

"So are you ready to drop that loser Reagan and come home with me?" she asked.

"Now, Hayden, you know how much I love your niece."

"Yes, she is one lucky woman."

"That she is, Hayden, and don't you forget it."

"You just be sure and tell her, one screw up and I am stepping in."

"She wants you over for dinner tomorrow night."

"What's for dessert?" Hayden asked with a devilish grin.

"I will fix your favorite, coconut cream pie."

"I will definitely be there."

"Tory is coming, too, so it will be just like the good old days." She grinned.

"Fantastic." Hayden dipped Julie.

"So who is the blonde devouring you with her eyes? She has been drooling ever since you stepped onto the dance floor."

"Just another straight girl who stumbles in from time to time, looking for a cheap thrill with a real lesbian." Hayden sighed. "She has been here for almost a month now."

"Another woman warm for your form, Hayden?"

"Very funny," Hayden said.

"So why not give her what she wants and send her on her way?"

Hayden's eyes were shining brightly at Julie. "Believe it or not I do have standards and I don't sleep with just anyone," she said, feigning a pout.

"I wouldn't say she was just anyone, the woman is drop-dead gorgeous," Julie prompted.

"And, if you haven't noticed, she is drop-dead straight. There isn't a lesbian cell in her body and I'll be damned if I am going there again."

Julie saw the excitement in Hayden's eyes shift to pain. "I am sorry I brought that up," she whispered, as she clung close to Hayden.

"I have to get over it eventually." The song ended and they walked back to the bar.

"You didn't tell me we were going for dinner tomorrow night," Hayden said to Tory.

"I don't have to tell you everything," Tory said with a smirk.

"Well what if I had plans for a date?"

"Then I would be your date." Tory winked at Julie. "You did tell her you were making her favorites, right?"

"Yes, you know that was the first thing she asked."

"You are so predictable, Hayden," Tory teased

Hayden was no longer listening her attention becoming captivated by the tall blonde woman approaching from across the bar.

"I will see you two tomorrow night. Right now I'm going to find Reagan," Julie said.

The new woman turned to Tory, her blue eyes sparkling. "Would you mind if I borrow your friend?" she asked in a soft, sultry voice.

"No, not at all."

The woman turned her eyes on Hayden. "Will you dance with me?"

"Sure." Hayden placed her drink on the bar and took the woman's offered hand.

The woman's skin was soft and warm to Hayden as she led them to the middle of the dance floor. "My name is Clarice," she said, as she turned to face Hayden.

"Nice to meet you, my name is Hayden."

"Yes, I know."

The music began to play a techno version of a popular song, a mix which Hayden recognized would last for almost eight minutes.

Her body picked up the rhythm quickly as she moved closer to her partner and locked eyes with her. The woman boldly matched Hayden's approach until their bodies were gyrating together as the music pounded out across the dance floor.

Hayden felt the heat building between them as she spun Clarice in her arms, her hips grinding into her ass as her hands circled the woman's waist. She could feel Clarice's body trembling beneath her hands as she buried her face in the woman's neck. The perfume she wore was intoxicating. Hayden breathed the scent deeply as her lips caressed the soft skin of Clarice's neck.

She moved her lips up to Clarice's neck and whispered in her ear. "What do you want?"

"I want you to open your heart to me and give me a chance."

Stunned by the woman's answer, Hayden's hands froze in place across Clarice's stomach as her words struck home. For a moment, Hayden felt her resolve melting. Then her thoughts returned to the humiliation she had felt the last time she fell for a straight woman. She spun Clarice around and looked directly into her eyes. They looked sincere, but Hayden refused to go there. Instead, she bent down and pressed her lips to Clarice's. The softness of her lips was tantalizing as they kissed, lightly at first. Clarice parted her lips and the kiss became urgent, passionate, and hungry. Hayden felt the vibration of a moan and she was unsure who issued the sound.

The song was ending as she broke the kiss. She cupped Clarice's chin in her hand, sang the last line of the song, *Baby, you're not the one for me,* spun on her heel, and stormed off the dance floor. She stopped at her barstool to retrieve her leather coat and quickly put it on.

Tory was looking up at her. "Are you okay?"

"I just need some fresh air. I will see you tomorrow night for the cookout." She walked away before Tory had a chance to reply.

Something was definitely not right with her friend and Tory turned to find Clarice standing on the dance floor with tears in her eyes. She felt bad for the woman and went to her. "Are you okay?"

Clarice looked at Tory and was able to shake her head before the tears began to fall. Tory took her hand and led her out a back door, past couples making out and into a small courtyard area. She sat Clarice at a table and held her hand while her tears fell.

When Clarice regained her composure, she looked at Tory with bleary eyes. "How can she be so cruel?"

"How was Hayden cruel?"

"She kissed me with so much passion and then bluntly stated that I wasn't the one for her." Clarice seemed to be fighting off her tears.

Tory brushed a strand of hair from Clarice's face. "Hayden has been my best friend for what seems like a lifetime and she is hurting. The last straight woman she became involved with hurt her very badly."

"How did she do that?"

"She enticed Hayden to her bed on a dare from her boyfriend and made a sex video without Hayden's consent."

"No wonder she has a hatred of women she assumes are straight."

"Hatred is a hard word, but Hayden has lost the ability to trust someone she does not know well. Are you saying you're not straight?"

"I am not sure what I am to be honest. I don't date men, but have never been with a woman either," Clarice answered honestly. She gave Tory a bashful smile. "The first time I came here and saw Hayden, I knew she was special, and for days afterward she was all I could talk about." Tory could see the blush growing brighter on her cheeks. "Cindy, the woman who comes with me is a co-worker who knows my desire to be with Hayden. She comes here to give me support and she encouraged me to approach Hayden."

"Oh man, this is so screwed up."

"I would never hurt Hayden or anyone else. I'm not like that woman."

"Hayden doesn't believe that and it will take a lot of effort to convince her otherwise."

"Do you think I would have any chance at changing her mind?"

"I honestly don't know." Tory fell silent in thought.

†

Hayden zipped up her jacket and mounted the bike. The engine roared to life and she sped away from the bar. It was late and most of the traffic lights had begun to flash and she was out of the city in minutes. She turned onto the Interstate and opened up the throttle. She leaned forward on the fast bike, the wind whipping through her dark hair as she rode aimlessly, trying to ease her mind. Tears had filled her eyes and the effect of the wind caused them to stream down her face. She had been mean to Clarice and was ashamed of herself for acting that way. She could not let Lauren's betrayal leave her so bitter and angry. She must find a way to let it go, she thought, as she raced down the empty road.

She cleared her mind and allowed the hum of the engine and the vibration of the powerful bike to take over her senses. As she rode, the vibrations from the bike, and flashes of Clarice's face began to overwhelm Hayden. An hour and two state lines later, Hayden pulled the bike to the side of the road and stopped. Her breathing had turned into panting as her body submitted to her need for a release of the sexual tension that had been building all night. She switched off the ignition and leaned forward across the bike to catch her breath and regain her composure. Her legs felt weak and she struggled to lower the kickstand just in case she could no longer support the weight of the bike. She could hear her heart still pounding in her ears as the quiet of the night set in.

Hayden was soaked. The intensity of the release had been one of the most powerful she had ever experienced and she had felt nothing like it on a solo journey before. When her breathing and pulse began to return to normal, Hayden pulled the bike back onto the Interstate and used the next exit to turn and head for home. The desire for a shower and her comfortable bed was calling her as she opened up the throttle, this time more cautious of the high speeds she had raced earlier.

When she finally pulled into her driveway, she realized how exhausted she had become, emotionally and physically. She shed clothes from the front door into her bedroom and stepped into the shower for a quick rinse. Her arms felt like lead as she dried her body, and when she collapsed onto the bed, Hayden was gone almost before her head touched her pillow.

The sun shining through her bedroom window woke Hayden the following morning. With sleepy eyes, she peeked at the clock to find it was already eleven. She couldn't believe how long she had slept. Maybe it was time for her to take a break from the bar and get some sleep on a Friday night. Other than getting some exercise and a few discouraging one night stands, the bar just made her feel lonely. Then there was Lauren, which had turned out a huge mistake.

She had no plans for the day until dinner at Julie's, so she pulled the sheet back over her head and went back to sleep.

When Hayden awoke hours later, she was starving. She dragged herself from the bed, threw on a robe and headed off in search of food. In the kitchen, she opened the refrigerator and pulled out a bowl of pasta that was only a day old, placing it in the microwave to heat while she poured herself a large glass of milk. She placed the milk on her small dining room table and returned to the kitchen for the dish, placing a large slice of butter over the steaming noodles.

She always looked forward to dinner at Julie and Reagan's. Her niece worked miracles at the grill while Julie prepared the inside foods. Tonight's menu of grilled chicken and fresh vegetables made her mouth water as she sat down to the leftover pasta. After she ate, she would shower and dress to go into town for a haircut. She could pick up a case of beer before returning home to prepare for her night out. Frequently, she, Reagan, and Tory drank too many beers, and she and Tory would end up on the couch or on a bed in the spare bedroom. Reagan was a city police officer and collected all keys as soon as her guests arrived.

†

Hayden finished her late lunch and placed her dishes in the dishwasher. She showered and walked back to her bedroom. The weather was still nice out, so she decided to wear shorts and a T-shirt into town. She grabbed the keys to her truck and walked out into the afternoon sun. After Hayden got her hair trimmed, she stopped by the grocery to pick up a case of beer and some ice, and placed them in the cooler in the back of her truck. She knew Reagan would already have beer on ice, but she always brought a case so no one would have to make a beer run if someone else stopped by.

The afternoon had flown past as Hayden rushed home to shower and dress for the evening out. Julie had not mentioned inviting anyone else, so Hayden decided to dress casually in well-worn jeans, leather loafers, and a form-fitting pullover. After a short spray of cologne, she was ready and slipped the keys to the truck into her pocket. As she walked back through the house, she stopped off at the kitchen to pick up one of Julie's favorite wines.

The fall sun was rapidly sinking into the horizon as she climbed into her truck and drove the short distance to Reagan and Julie's. When she pulled into the drive, she found Tory's car parked. She grabbed the wine and walked into the house. Tory and Reagan would already be in the back yard so Hayden would grab Tory to help her carry in the beer. As

11

luck would have it, Julie was in the kitchen checking on some dish when Hayden walked in. She snuck over and hugged Julie from behind and kissed her neck.

"Hello, Hayden."

"Hey there, my lovely, I brought something just for you." She handed Julie the bottle of wine.

"You always know how to treat a lady." Julie took the wine, examined the label, and smiled.

"Don't I wish that were true, then I would be bringing a lady and not just a bottle of wine."

"Who knows, maybe you will find someone soon who will put up with you. After all, Reagan found me, so there is hope for you yet."

"Is she out back with Tory?" Hayden looked out the window. "I need someone to help me carry in the cooler." Hayden saw three women in the back yard and strained her eyes to get a better view of the third person. "What the hell?"

"It is a long story, but one you need to hear."

"I am not sure I want to hear it," Hayden said. "I don't have the time or energy for that."

"Just trust me, be patient, and hear her out," Julie stopped Hayden in her tracks. Hayden had already started walking toward the front door.

"Stay here and I will get Tory to help you with the cooler." Julie left the house.

Hayden felt her cheeks flushing with anger as Tory walked toward the house. "What the fuck are you thinking, bringing her here?" she demanded when Tory walked in.

"Excuse me, but I had Julie's permission to bring a guest, your highness," Tory quipped seemingly perturbed by Hayden's attitude.

"I'm sorry, but I wasn't expecting to find her here, and especially brought by my best friend."

"If I weren't your best friend I would just let her think of you as the cruel ass you acted like last night. We made some terrible assumptions about Clarice, and if nothing else, I think you owe it to her to hear her out before you storm out rudely again."

Fully chastised by her friend, Hayden backed down. "Come help me with the cooler and you can tell me more of what is going on."

Tory followed her out to the truck. Hayden lowered the tailgate and pulled the cooler toward them, taking two beers out and twisting the tops off. She handed one to Tory and sat back on the tailgate. "So talk to me."

"Well after you stormed out last night, leaving Clarice standing alone in tears on the dance floor, I took her outside to console her. She is not at all what you believe her to be."

"I'm listening," Hayden sipped her beer.

"I am not going to tell you everything, but just that you need to talk to her."

"You certainly seem determined, so why don't you pursue her if she is so interesting?"

"Hayden, sometimes you can be such a dick. That woman only has eyes for you, though I don't know why she would bother to fall for such an arrogant ass."

"Ouch. That's a bit intense."

"You should hear yourself sometimes, Hayden. For just a minute, think of someone else's feelings. If I didn't love you like a sister, I don't know if I would bother," Tory said harshly.

Hayden swallowed hard. She knew that Tory was right, but she was so scared of getting hurt again that she had become calloused and bitter.

"So what would you have me do?"

"Carry this cooler out to the patio for me, then grab two beers and ask Clarice if she would like to go for a walk.

13

There is that nice little gazebo that overlooks the lake that would make a great location to have a private talk."

"Yes, there is that," Hayden said.

"You should at least hear her out."

"Yes, dear," Hayden said as she stepped off the tailgate. "No time like the present, so grab that end will you?"

†

They carried the cooler around to the back of the house and Hayden reached in for three beers. "Hey Romeo," she said to Reagan as she passed her a beer.

"Hey, Hayden, I think you know Clarice," Reagan said, as she took the beer and offered Hayden a smile.

"Yes, we have met. How are you tonight?"

"I am good thanks, and you?"

"I am good, too. Reagan would you mind if I borrow Clarice for a bit?"

"Just don't forget to bring her back when the food is ready," Reagan said.

Hayden turned back to Clarice. "Will you walk with me?" she asked, handing her a beer.

"Yes, I would like that."

Clarice turned and followed Hayden toward the lake.

"You look very nice tonight."

"Thank you," Clarice replied, blushing slightly.

"I guess I should start by apologizing for being such an ass last night."

"That would be a good place to start," Clarice said, not willing to let Hayden off the hook.

They reached the gazebo and Hayden offered Clarice a seat. "I apologize for my behavior last night. It was completely uncalled for."

"Yes, it was, but after talking with Tory, I understand why you could feel that way."

"Still, I cannot hold everyone accountable for the actions of one woman and I must learn to deal with that before it destroys me."

"Agreed, but I think I need to explain some things to you as well."

Hayden was fidgeting nervously in her seat.

"I am not the straight woman you think I am."

"Oh really," Hayden smirked.

"There you go again, being an ass." Clarice glared at her.

Hayden reeled back from her rebuff. Clarice was right she was being an ass and didn't even realize how she was coming across. "Sorry."

"That's two strikes already," Clarice teased. "But anyhow, no, I am not the straight woman out to mess with a lesbian's head with a bunch of games."

"So, why do you and your friend continue coming back?"

"My friend, Cindy, has been my support system as I have discovered my attraction to women, more specifically to you."

Hayden felt her cheeks grow hot as she listened to Clarice.

"Cindy and I work together and have been best friends for years, just like you and Tory. Yes, she is married with kids, but has been the one person in my life who doesn't think I have suddenly become mentally unstable."

"That is debatable if you are still interested in me." Hayden laughed.

"I am beginning to wonder about that myself," Clarice answered without cracking a smile. "Anyhow, when I first told Cindy I was attracted to women, she suggested we go out to the bar. When I first saw you, I knew you were someone very special."

"That is where you are wrong, I am just me."

"Arrogant and obstinate, yes, but the women flock to you and fight for your attention. There is no way every woman in the bar can be so wrong about your charisma."

Hayden blushed furiously and lowered her head. She still had some modesty after all.

"The feelings I experienced watching you terrified me at first, but after a week's worth of encouragement from Cindy, I was convinced that I had to meet you." Clarice took a deep breath before she continued. "When I finally had the courage to approach you last night, and we danced, my body was trembling so hard with excitement I could hardly breathe."

Tory joined Reagan back out on the patio. "Hey, Reagan, how does it seem to be going?"

"Well, Hayden is still sitting there listening and hasn't stormed off yet, so it must be going well. I really think Clarice is someone special. She seems to be nice. There is no doubt she is smitten with my dear aunt. Did you see the way she looked at Hayden?"

"It is hard to miss. When they were out on the dance floor last night, you could feel the chemistry between them and I think it scared Hayden."

"Hayden, scared of a woman? That's a new one."

"Maybe not the woman, but definitely how the woman made her feel," Tory clarified. "When Hayden left the bar last night, there was a look in her eyes I haven't seen for months."

"You think Romeo has finally met her Juliet?"

Tory shrugged. "I think it is a possibility."

Julie walked out of the house and joined them. "How is dinner coming?"

"The chicken has been done for a few minutes. I am just keeping it warm until we are prepared to eat."

Julie chuckled. "I'm ready, so I hope those two will finish up their little chat soon."

Hayden looked away from Clarice back toward the house and saw the small group hovering around the grill.

"What is it you want?" Hayden asked for the second time.

"The same thing I asked you for last night, for you to open your heart and give me the chance."

"I am not sure my heart is ready for that," Hayden said.

"I am a patient person and will give you all the time you need to decide. I just want a chance to prove to you who I really am."

"Can you deal with arrogant and obstinate?"

"I like to think I can."

"So let's take it slow. If something other than a friendship grows, then it was meant to be."

"I think that's a good idea." Hayden glanced over Clarice's shoulder. "I think I can hear Julie's stomach growling from here. We need to get back so we can eat." Hayden stood and offered her hand to Clarice. "I would like to give you a ride home tonight and maybe we can make some other plans, for a day at the beach or some other activity."

"I would like that." Clarice took Hayden's hand.

"Thank you."

"For what?"

"For forgiving me for being an ass."

"I haven't quite forgiven you yet." Clarice grinned. "That too will take time."

†

Hayden drank beer during and after dinner while Clarice helped Julie drink the bottle of wine. She had promised to give Clarice a ride home, so she limited herself to be able to safely drive. The dinner had gone well and she found Tory grinning at her several times during dessert as Clarice's hand rested comfortably on Hayden's thigh.

Before the night grew long, Hayden stood to say her goodbyes. "I promised Clarice a ride home, so stay and enjoy your night, Tory."

"That's fine. Are you okay to drive?" she asked.

"There is plenty of room if you two would like to stay," Julie said.

"I am fine. I promise to call you when I get home, okay?" she teased Julie.

"Thank you for a great meal and a wonderful evening," Clarice said to Julie and Reagan. Then she turned to Tory and kissed her cheek. "Thank you for bringing me."

"You are very welcome."

"Goodnight ladies," Hayden said as she reached for Clarice's hand and lead her out of the house.

"Does anyone else know what is wrong with this picture? I bring a woman to a party and Hayden leaves with her. That is so not right," Tory said with a chuckle.

"You know exactly what you are doing, Tory, and I appreciate you looking out for Hayden," Reagan said. "Sometimes, she just doesn't know what's good for her."

"That's for damned sure." Tory laughed. "Would you like another beer?"

"You sit and I will get it," Julie said.

†

Hayden opened the truck door for Clarice and got her settled inside before walking around to climb in behind the wheel. "Where to?" she asked.

Clarice gave her the general direction and then pointed out a very nice two-story house at the end of a secluded block. "Would you like to come in?"

"No, but I will walk you to the door." Hayden walked around and opened the door for Clarice. "What would you like to do tomorrow?"

"Surprise me."

"Okay, dress comfortably then." As they walked to the door, Clarice fished her keys from her pocket.

"Are you sure you won't come in?"

"Thanks, but not tonight."

"Very well then..." She was about to say something else when Hayden pulled her close and softly kissed her. She could taste the sweet wine as her tongue penetrated Clarice's lips and swirled inside her mouth. Clarice's hands moved down Hayden's hips and pulled her in tighter. Hayden wanted this woman and the way she kissed made her want her even more. A soft moan escaped her.

Hayden broke the kiss with a sweet smile. "I will see you in the morning about ten, if that's okay."

"That will be fine."

"Goodnight, Clarice."

"Goodnight, Hayden."

Hayden walked back to her truck and sat watching until Clarice disappeared inside the house to start the engine and pull away.

†

The feel of Hayden's body remained with Clarice as she climbed the stairs to her bedroom and stripped out of her clothing. She noticed her panties were soaked as she removed them and climbed between the sheets. She touched herself, amazed at how wet she was. She reached to her nightstand to pull out a vibrator. She used the toy to relieve her tension and called out Hayden's name as her climax surged through her.

†

Hayden drove the short distance to her apartment, planning tomorrow's trip with Clarice. She would pack a picnic lunch and a bottle of wine and take Clarice for a ride to the beach. She pulled into her drive, making a mental note to go to the store for supplies first thing in the morning. She parked and went inside to fall into an exhausted sleep as soon as her head touched her pillow. Sweet images of Clarice filled her dreams as the night fell away.

The next morning she woke early and drove to the grocery store to pick up supplies. Hayden made small finger sandwiches and filled a container with them. She also packaged fresh fruit and chips and packed them away in a backpack along with the bottle of wine, a corkscrew, two cocktail glasses, and a sheet. As an afterthought, she also tossed in a light sweatshirt in case Clarice got cold.

She showered and dressed in jeans and a black tank top then pulled on a black oxford to layer her clothing. It was still warm, but Hayden knew that the weather at the beach could change quickly. After a misting of cologne, Hayden picked up the backpack and walked out to her bike. She secured an extra helmet on the back, slung the backpack over her shoulders, and mounted the bike.

The drive to Clarice's home passed quickly. She pulled up in the drive and turned off the bike. Clarice met her at the front door, dressed in jeans and a thin blouse. Hayden smiled when she saw Clarice. "I think you might want a heavier top."

"I think you are right. Come on in and I'll find something."

Hayden stepped inside and closed the door. "How are you doing today?"

"I am great thanks. I had a wonderful night's sleep. How about you?"

"I slept like a rock."

"Make yourself comfortable and I'll be right back." Hayden looked around and walked into a well-decorated living room to take a seat in a heavy leather chair. She sank deeply into the luxurious chair as she looked around the room. A flat-screen television and high-tech sound system were the features of the room. Ansel Adams prints covered the walls and the room held a warm, lived-in feel to it. She looked over at a long leather couch and could easily imagine Clarice lying here at night, watching television or listening to music. Hayden was deep in thought when Clarice entered the room.

"I hope this is better?"

Hayden stood to turn toward Clarice who had changed into a light sweater with a T-shirt beneath it. "That should do. You look very nice."

"Thank you. You look rather handsome yourself," Clarice stepped forward to softly kiss Hayden. "I am ready if you are."

Hayden followed Clarice out the front door to the bike. She had placed the backpack on the ground. "I hope you won't mind wearing this while we ride."

"No, not at all."

Hayden took the spare helmet and placed it on Clarice's head. "This should do," she buckled the helmet.

Hayden mounted the bike and turned to offer Clarice a hand. Clarice climbed onto the bike easily. "You have ridden before haven't you?"

"Yes, a guy I dated in High School had a bike."

"Good. So you know to relax and wrap your arms around me."

"I think I can handle that." Clarice leaned forward and wrapped her arms around Hayden's waist.

"That's good." Hayden started the ignition and made a U-turn in the drive. After several minutes of riding, she felt Clarice's grip on her body relax as she got used to riding with Hayden.

Hayden sped up and took turns and curves gently as they rode toward the coast. She passed the main entrance, driving on to a more isolated section of the beach.

When she was satisfied she was at the right spot, Hayden pulled into a small parking cove and turned off the bike.

Clarice carefully dismounted and stood beside it as Hayden dropped the kickstand to secure the bike.

"That was a great ride, Hayden. I had forgotten how much fun a bike could be."

"I love to ride, especially on the weekends after all the tourists have left for the season."

Hayden took the backpack and threw it over her shoulder. "It is a bit of a walk, but the view is worth it."

"No problem. It's a beautiful day."

Hayden reached for Clarice's hand and they began walking down a pathway. When they reached the beach, Hayden pointed toward a small section of dunes that jutted out toward the water. They would have some protection from the wind that was blowing steadily down the beach.

When they reached the dunes, Hayden took off the backpack. She pulled out the sheet and with Clarice's help spread it across the soft sand. "Are you hungry?" she asked as they settled in on the sheet.

"A little." Hayden reached into the backpack and pulled out the glasses and the bottle of wine. She handed the bottle to Clarice and dug into the pack for the corkscrew. "You can open this while I prepare lunch."

Clarice took the corkscrew and began opening the bottle of wine as Hayden took the fruit, chips, and sandwiches from the backpack.

"This looks great." Clarice worked the cork from the bottle. She poured them glasses of wine and handed one to Hayden.

"Thanks. I thought this would make a simple meal for us to share on the beach."

Warmed by the smile Clarice gave her, Hayden said, "You have a beautiful house, do you mind if I ask what you do?"

"No, not at all. I am a dentist, just opening my own practice."

"Do I need to call you 'Doctor' then?" Hayden winked.

"No, Clarice will do just fine."

Hayden picked up a sandwich.

"So what do you do, Hayden?"

"I am a bean counter."

"An accountant, hmm, I wouldn't have thought that."

"Why not?"

"Well you don't have that nerdy accountant profile."

"Hey, that's a stereotype. We have moved beyond."

"Oh, is it?"

"Yes, ma'am, I lost the black-rimmed glasses and pocket protector years ago."

"Would you be interested in doing my books? I am looking for a good accountant."

"I think I might be able to arrange a look at them. I have a pretty busy schedule, but I'm sure I can squeeze you in."

"I would appreciate that. I would like to have someone I could trust."

"Are you accepting new patients?"

"Yes, I have room for at least one more. You have beautiful teeth by the way. Sorry, it's a habit of dentists to notice teeth first."

Hayden laughed softly. "Why thank you, ma'am."

"This is very good wine. Is it the same as the one you brought to Julie's last night?"

"It is the same brand, but a different vintage."

"I really like your taste in wine."

"I don't drink it often, but I like good wine when I do."

"Maybe you can take me shopping for some. I really like this." Clarice raised her glass and took another sip.

"I think that could be arranged."

They made small talk throughout the rest of the meal. They had drunk half of the bottle and Hayden felt the warm glow from the sweet wine.

"Would you like to take a walk?"

"Yes, I would love to." The wind and the wine had put a blush to her cheeks.

"Are you warm enough?" Hayden asked.

"Yes, I am fine."

Hayden once more reached for Clarice's hand. When she took it, she entwined her fingers with Clarice's and felt the soft, warm skin press into her palm. They walked for nearly an hour, stopping along the way to look at shells that had washed up on the beach or to marvel at a group of dolphins that played in the breakers.

Hayden noticed threatening clouds starting to appear. "I think we might want to head back. It looks like our weather is changing."

Clarice looked at the dark clouds that were forming. "Let's go back to my place and finish the wine."

†

They walked quickly back to their spot in the dunes and packed up their supplies as the wind began to whip around them. They mounted, and the vibration of the bike again seduced Clarice, as Hayden raced the rain back to the house. The powerful vibrations and the feel of Hayden so close heightened the intoxicating measure of the wine. When they reached her home, Clarice was ready to ravish Hayden. She climbed off the bike and told Hayden to pull in the garage, just as raindrops were beginning to fall. She activated a remote pad and the garage door lifted.

Hayden pulled into the garage beside a convertible BMW Z 4. She parked the bike and smiled at Clarice. "Nice ride." She took a closer look at the car.

"Thanks, I love it."

Hayden followed Clarice into the kitchen from the garage.

"Take a look around while I pour us a glass of wine."

Hayden walked through the kitchen filled with stainless steel appliances into a family room that led out to a large yard with a covered pool and patio. "Nice back yard."

Clarice walked up beside her, holding the bottle and two glasses of wine.

"Thanks. I love sitting out by the pool and listening to the sound of the rain falling."

"Should we go there now?"

"I do have a very comfortable chaise lounge."

"Big enough for two?"

"Most definitely."

"What are we waiting for then?" Hayden opened the door.

Hayden followed Clarice out to the pool and watched as she set the wine on the table and slipped her loafers off. Hayden sat down and took off her boots then joined Clarice on the lounge. Hayden sank into luxurious comfort as she sat back and placed her left arm around Clarice's shoulder. She took a glass of wine and enjoyed a sip.

"This is perfect," Hayden said as the raindrops began falling in earnest on the aluminum roof.

Clarice snuggled into Hayden's body. "It is so relaxing."

Hayden reached over Clarice to place her wine glass on the table. She could feel the warmth of her body as Clarice pressed in close and looked in her eyes to find them sparkling with excitement. She watched as the tip of Clarice's tongue snaked out across her lips in anticipation of a kiss.

She smiled and took Clarice's face in her hands and lowered her mouth to brush her lips across Clarice's. Clarice moaned and used her free hand to pull Hayden's head down for a firmer kiss as she opened her lips in invitation.

Hayden shifted her body to face Clarice, her fingers stroking down Clarice's face. She opened her mouth and tasted the sweet wine still lingering on Clarice's lips as their tongues met and swirled together in a seductive dance. She fell captive to the allure of Clarice. Hayden inhaled deeply, savoring the scent of her perfume. The rain intensified, drowning out their moans as the kiss grew from lingering teasing to a passionate exploration of one another.

Clarice's hand slowly caressed down Hayden's back down to her hips where she found her belt and pulled her closer until Hayden's hips rested on top of her. The weight of Hayden's body sent shivers through her as the kiss ignited a passion deep inside. Clarice found herself shaking uncontrollably with her desire for Hayden.

When Clarice pulled her so she was laying on top of her, Hayden felt their encounter spiraling out of control. She could not deny her attraction to Clarice, as her lust rushed through her veins, but she wasn't entirely sure they were ready to move forward. The quivering of Clarice's body beneath her added to her confusion, her body screaming to be naked and wrapped in Clarice's arms.

Clarice's hands worked to pull Hayden's shirt out of her jeans. Her fingers ached to touch Hayden's skin and once she had pulled the shirt out, they roamed all over her back, her nails stirring up trails of shivers through Hayden.

Sounds of thunder in the distance signaled the approaching storm. Hayden's body moved with a will of its own as her hips began to slowly grind into Clarice as their bodies began to melt together. Clarice's hands moved down to cover Hayden's ass, pulling her in deeper.

Her imaginary line of restraint crossed, Hayden allowed her hand to slip between them and begin kneading Clarice's breast.

Clarice broke off the kiss to whisper breathlessly to Hayden. "I need you."

Hayden looked into Clarice's eyes, finding them filled with a dark hunger. She moved to straddle her waist, and reached down and pulled the sweater over Clarice's head.

Clarice reached behind her back to remove her bra. In the dim light of the falling evening, Hayden looked down and saw milky white, perfectly shaped breasts.

She leaned forward and kissed down Clarice's neck as her hand caressed the soft mounds of flesh that were heaving up to meet her touch with each of Clarice's ragged breaths. Her nipples were fully erect, begging for a kiss, and Hayden was fully up to the task. She moved down between Clarice's legs and took a breast in her mouth as her hand continued to tease and stroke her body.

The feel of Hayden's hot, wet mouth on her breast had a profound effect. Clarice felt her dampness seeping through her clothes as her hands struggled to lift Hayden's shirt. She desperately needed to feel Hayden's skin on hers. Frustrated that she could only lift the shirt a short distance, she broke the silence. "Take this off please, Hayden. I need to feel you next to me."

Hayden paused in her sucking to quickly unbutton her shirt and drop it to the floor. Clarice pulled the tank top over her head and then pulled Hayden down to finally feel their skin touch. "Oh God, yes," she murmured. As Hayden's mouth returned to her breast, she could feel firm nipples dragging across her skin.

She softly raked Hayden's back with her fingertips as Hayden's mouth brought her previously unknown pleasure.

Hayden's hand moved down between them to come to rest on the hot center of Clarice. She could feel the wetness through the jeans as she cupped her mound and gave it a soft squeeze. Hayden's hand deftly unfastened the belt and opened the front of Clarice's jeans, revealing soft skin and lacy panties. Clarice lifted her hips to allow Hayden to pull the jeans off, leaving her panties in place for the moment. Hayden changed breasts while her fingertips circled Clarice's soaked lips through her panties. Clarice's hips strained to press her wetness into Hayden's hand, while her own hand worked to unfasten Hayden's belt.

Hayden stopped her movement long enough to pause to remove her jeans and socks, leaving her naked before Clarice's eyes that were busy ravishing her body. She leaned down to remove Clarice's panties and then lay down on top of her, skin on skin, as their mouths joined again.

Clarice wrapped her legs around Hayden's, her hands urgently pulling her hips as Hayden started to grind into her.

For hours, their bodies enjoyed every touch, kiss, lick, and bite, until they ended up in a sweat-covered pile on the chaise, utterly exhausted. The rain continued pounding on the roof, flashes of lightning illuminating their features, as they lay entwined. Time had become meaningless and it was apparent that the weather would prevent Hayden from going home, so they rested together until the night began to turn cool.

"Why don't we go to my bedroom," Clarice suggested.

They picked up their pile of clothes and made a dash for the house through the pouring rain. Hayden followed Clarice up the stairs to her bedroom and dropped her clothing on the floor.

"I could use a shower," Hayden said.

"Let's rinse off then before we get some rest," Clarice said. She took Hayden to the shower and then after they had dried, invited her to her bed.

Their bodies were exhausted from lovemaking, but the two lovers shared long tender kisses and soft caresses before Clarice snuggled into Hayden's arms. Within minutes, both women had drifted off to sleep and slept soundly until the alarm sounded several hours later.

Clarice reached over to silence it and turned back to Hayden. She brushed a lock of hair from her face and leaned down to softly kiss her lips. "Thank you for yesterday."

"My pleasure."

"Mine too, several times in fact."

With a deep sigh, Hayden climbed from the bed and began dressing to return home to shower and prepare for work.

"Will you call me this week, Hayden?"

"How about tonight?"

"That would be perfect. I know we could both use a full night's sleep, so how about coming over for dinner Tuesday?"

"Tuesday sounds great." Hayden slipped on her boots and walked around the bed to take Clarice in her arms.

Still naked from their slumber, Clarice's body sent a surge of excitement racing through Hayden as her bare breasts pressed into her chest.

"I am tempted to call in to work and take you back to bed to ravage you all day, but I am sure you have a busy schedule today, too."

"Keep that thought in mind for tomorrow night, and maybe we will skip dinner and go straight to dessert," Clarice said.

"Maybe I should bring a change of clothes."

"I think that would be wise. At least we could wake up together and prepare for work at a normal time."

Hayden leaned down to kiss her deeply, her hands roaming over Clarice's body. "I better get moving. Will you follow me down and close the garage?"

Hayden took the opportunity to kiss each nipple before Clarice covered them with a robe to follow her downstairs. After a final kiss, Hayden walked out to the garage to mount the bike and head for home.

She turned her head at the end of the drive to see Clarice watching her and lifted her hand in a wave before speeding out to the street. The crisp morning air greeted her and she felt the best she had in a long time as she twisted the bike around curves. Maybe Clarice was the one she waited for. The night had gone very well and she felt a connection with Clarice. She shook her head when she realized how close she had been to walking away from someone who really seemed to care for her.

She made a mental note to call Tory and thank her for being a great friend. If she hadn't been persistent, Hayden would have missed out on someone very special. She pulled into her drive and felt her phone vibrating in her pocket.

She answered the phone to find Clarice on the other end.

"I miss you already."

Hayden softly chuckled. "Do you want to come over tonight?"

"Yes."

"Call me when you get home and I will give you directions. I will pick up some Chinese and we can crash and watch a movie."

"That sounds great, Hayden. Have a good day."

"You too, Clarice." Hayden closed her phone. She stepped inside her apartment feeling like a brand new woman.

The Dreamer

"Good night and sweet dreams," is our usual farewell to end our conversation, but tonight it was destined to be the beginning of something more. I pulled the T-shirt over my head and stepped out of the shorts I was wearing and climbed the steps to my bed. Lying naked on my back, my arms, and legs spread, a sheet barely covering my nakedness from the waist down, my mind began to relax. Listening to the softly falling rain, sleep became a blessing and quickly ushered my mind into the realm of dreams.

I was completely relaxed when I felt the bed shift from the weight of your body as you climbed in next to me and lay beside me. I kept my eyes closed tightly in fear of losing the dream if I allowed them to open, and I awaited your touch.

I felt your delicate fingertips as they gently caressed my arm and I struggled to suppress a soft moan. Then your tongue began at the inside of my wrist and slowly bathed my skin as you licked up the length of my arm. A shiver ran through me as your tongue reached the top of my shoulder and continued toward my neck.

I felt you shift on the bed, your heated skin pressed against my side as your tongue continued its journey. I feel the warmth of your breath against my skin and as your tongue dipped into my ear. I felt the throbbing of desire building in my loins. I burned for your touch and quivered at the very thought of your kisses.

"I want you," I imagined you breathing those words into my ear, but it was only an echo in my mind. Your voice remained silent as your body communicated its desire. I felt your hand graze over my left breast and my nipple rose to kiss the softness of your palm. They ached for your touch and your warm mouth and you were more than willing to oblige. Your fingertips lightly traced the sides of my nipples making each grow to nearly painful hardness as your lips tugged at my earlobe. The veins leading to my nipples swelled to fullness as your nails traced their paths as they rushed blood to my throbbing flesh.

The searing heat of your body next to mine melted the last remnants of my restraint, and I felt the flow of excitement trickle past my swollen lips. Your head lowered and I felt the puffs of your heated breaths against the mound of my right breast as you filled your mouth with excited flesh.

I raised my hand to gently stroke the silky hair from around your face as your mouth sucked greedily. Your hair fell from your shoulders and licked my skin as your tongue and teeth teased my nipple. My hands explored down your back, the smoothness of your skin feeling like velvet to my fingertips. My nails unconsciously graze your back; as they caress you the vibration of your moan resonates against my breast.

Your hand lowers to take the thin sheet in your grasp, as you pull the covering off my body revealing my nakedness. Your hand brushes the inside of my thigh, I

33

quiver with delight as your fingers brush the dew soaked hairs nestled between my trembling legs. Your hand caresses the softness of my stomach as your mouth transfers to encircle my left breast.

My body is sweltering with need as your mouth entices moans that I can no longer restrain and I hear them echo throughout the room. My hands urge you closer and I feel the weight of you as you lower yourself onto me. You remove your mouth from my breast as I feel your wetness press deeply between my thighs.

I feel your breath on my face as you lower your mouth to mine, and press your tongue between my lips. We share the taste of the kiss as the fruit of our passion entwines with our tongues to dance seductively in our hungry mouths. My hands cup the cheeks of your ass, and I can feel the rippling of muscles as your hips grind slowly into my body and I pull you deeper into me. My body surrenders to your domination as you control the rhythms of our bodies and you seduce me so completely. You take my small hands in one of your larger ones and pin them above my head forbidding me to touch your body as your mouth threatens to steal the breath from my body with fevered kisses.

The movement of your hips forces my thighs to spread further, bringing your body to rest completely on mine as your hardened clit slides the length of my swollen lips as the friction between us erodes. You glide smoothly up to my pulsing clit and as they dance together, I gasp for breath buried in your mouth and you relent allowing me a breath as you bury your face in my neck. My hands struggle to be free, to push you further down my body, but you hold them firmly in place as you torture my body with sensual kisses. You will take me at your leisure and your soft chuckle as I struggle confirms your intent to me. Your teeth find my sensitive lobe and I feel my breathing grow rapid as you breathe deeply in my ear.

I attempt to roll my hips into yours as the heat continues to build between us, and your hips drive our bodies into the mattress. Your left hand cups my right breast as your tongue traps my nipple against the roof of your mouth and you pull gently as I arch my back into you. Your strong fingers knead my breast as your teeth lightly nip at my swollen nipples. I can feel a drop of perspiration fall from your face as your mouth moves in a slow descent down my body and the droplet trickles down my side to evaporate into the sheet. Your nipples drag across the softness of my stomach, and I can feel the arousal in your hardened peaks as they draw across my groin.

My hands are finally released, and I bury them in your silky hair as it cascades over my skin. Your breath is on fire as you move between my thighs, and I can hear your labored breathing for the first time. Your fingertips gently part my swollen lips and you flatten your tongue in the outer layers of aroused flesh to lap the juice that has escaped my well. You breathe deeply of the aroma and then penetrate me with your tongue, probing intensely as your elbows keep my thighs spread wide. My entire body shivers uncontrollably as your mouth covers me completely. Your tongue curls inside, licking my walls as I begin to shudder. Your tongue slides in and out of me as my hips thrust wildly against your face and you replace your tongue with three long fingers that drive into me as your mouth covers my clit in a deep soul kiss. Your fingers explore and find every spot that turns my body into a writhing mass of limbs and flesh as you bring me to peak after peak of climax.

After a final shudder of release, you move back up my body and we share one final kiss. The taste of passion explodes between us and your hips grind into me as you release your pleasure. The intensity of your climax is so magnificent that my eyes open wide, and I find I am alone in the bed, my body soaked and shivering from the aftereffects of the lovemaking.

My hand gropes down the bed until it locates the sheet and tucking it neatly under my chin, I close my eyes in hope of finding you again in my dreams.

The Perfect Gift

Adrianna Cooper was hours away from her thirtieth birthday when she received a call from her friend and coworker, Marcus. She had known him for nearly ten years and they had become close friends. At five-feet ten inches tall, Adrianna could look at Marcus squarely with her icy blue eyes, and she would never back down from his constant teasing.

They worked at the same stock brokerage house during the day, and at night, they enjoyed dominating their female sexual partners. Marcus had tried for years to find the perfect slave for Adrianna but, so far, she had not taken a serious interest in any of the women he had provided.

Her current submissive was the beautiful Monique. While the sex was enjoyable, the chemistry had not developed between them. Monique worshipped her Mistress, but it wasn't enough, so Adrianna had asked Marcus to find a good Mistress for her. So far, he had not located someone that suited Adrianna's requirements. She would only release Monique to someone she thought worthy of such a beautiful slave. Until Marcus found the right Mistress, Monique would continue to serve Adrianna, the woman she adored.

Adrianna had just retired to her bedroom for the evening when Monique knocked on the bedroom door. After her command to enter, Monique arrived carrying a portable telephone.

"Master Marcus is on the telephone for you, Mistress." She handed Adrianna the telephone.

"Thank you, Monique. Leave us and come back in fifteen minutes.

"Yes, Mistress." Monique gave a slight bow and left the room.

"Hello, Marcus."

"Cooper, my dear," Marcus greeted with a chuckle.

Marcus was the only person allowed to address Adrianna by her last name. He took advantage of this privilege whenever he could.

"How are you Marcus?"

"I am fine, my friend. I was calling to inform you that we have plans for your birthday tomorrow night."

"Do tell." Adrianna's interest was piqued by the tone in his voice.

"We are going to the Pit tomorrow night to pick up your birthday present." The Pit was a local leather bar that catered to an elite crowd.

"The Pit, huh? What kind of present should I expect this year?"

"The perfect gift. You will learn exactly what it is at eight tomorrow night, love. See you tomorrow at work," Marcus said, and then the telephone went dead.

Adrianna laid the telephone on the nightstand and relaxed against the pillows on the bed. A few moments later, Monique knocked and entered. She walked over to Adrianna and knelt at the side of the bed. She lowered her eyes. "How may I serve you tonight, Mistress?"

"Strip for me," Adrianna commanded.

Monique stood and opened the belt of her Kimono robe and allowed the silky material to fall to the floor. Adrianna watched as Monique slid the spaghetti straps of the black teddy over her shoulders and slowly peeled the soft fabric down and off her body.

Monique's breasts were full and round, her nipples pierced with gold rings. Adrianna smiled as they grew to firm peaks under her gaze. Her eyes continued down Monique's body to come to rest on the freshly shaved mound between her long legs.

"Bring me my crop," she instructed.

Monique walked to the dresser and opened the top drawer. She reached inside the drawer filled with pleasure items and withdrew a black, braided-leather crop.

Adrianna watched Monique walk back to the bed carrying the prized object. There was a glint of excitement in her dark eyes as she offered the crop to her Mistress.

"Lie across the bed on your back," Adrianna said as she sat up.

Monique laid her body across the end of the bed as instructed and waited eagerly for her next command.

Adrianna used the flared tip of the crop to gently caress down Monique's neck, down across her collarbone, and finally across her swollen nipples. She flicked the gold rings back and forth with the tip of the crop and a small moan of pleasure escaped Monique's lips.

"Quiet," Adrianna barked as the tip of the crop smacked against Monique's throbbing left nipple. A red mark raised on the soft skin and Adrianna glared her disapproval.

"Spread your legs," she commanded with a sharp blow to Monique's right thigh.

Monique spread her legs as instructed, her body trembling with excitement. She watched with expectation as the tip of the crop descended her body, and then disappeared between her spread thighs. The soft leather must feel delicious against her bare lips because she stifled a deep moan, fearful of angering her Mistress again.

"Spread your lips," Adrianna said.

Monique brought her hands between her thighs. Her fingers gently spread the lips of her sex, exposing the pink flesh to the black leather of the crop.

Adrianna stroked the tip of the crop down her lips and the braided sections of the crop caressed Monique's damp folds. She tapped the flared end against Monique's swollen clit and smiled as her body squirmed on the bed.

"Do you know what I think?" Adrianna growled; desire saturated her voice.

"What, Mistress?"

"I believe you need to be fucked."

"Oh yes, Mistress, please."

"Prepare me then," Adrianna rose to stand next to the bed.

Monique moved quickly from the bed and returned to the dresser. She opened the drawer and pulled out a black leather harness and a large dildo. She carried them over to the bed and opened Adrianna's robe with trembling hands. She placed the harness at her Mistress's feet and waited for her to step into the openings, then carefully raised the harness up her Mistress's legs and fastened it firmly around her waist. Once the harness was snug, she reached for the dildo and slid it onto the harness ring.

"Now get it wet."

Monique remained on her knees and took the dildo in her small hands. She began at the head and caressed the length of the dildo with her tongue. Adrianna slapped the crop against each of her ass cheeks, raising small welts. Monique opened her mouth and took as much of the dildo in as she could tolerate without gagging.

"That's right, suck it good." A second round of blows smacked across Monique's ass.

Adrianna grabbed a handful of Monique's hair, tilted her head backward until her dark lust-filled eyes stared into Adrianna's icy blues.

"Are you ready to be fucked?"

Monique nodded her head yes and Adrianna pointed to the full-length mirror. Monique slid the dildo from her mouth, walked across the room, and straddled the small ottoman positioned in front of the mirror. Monique spread her legs and raised her hips as she offered herself to her Mistress.

Adrianna walked over and placed the dildo between Monique's swollen lips. "Hold it until you are ready," she instructed.

Monique's right hand held the heavy dildo against her lips as her Mistress began to rock her hips, coating it with Monique's juices. Monique spread her lips with her fingers and positioned the head of the dildo at her opening. Adrianna penetrated her slowly, until the full length disappeared inside Monique.

"Does this feel good?"

"Oh yes, Mistress, it does." Adrianna slowly withdrew almost the entire length and began thrusting into Monique's hips, rocking her body with each slap of her thighs against Monique's ass.

The pressure of the harness straps against her clit was highly pleasurable to Adrianna as she continued to stroke deep inside Monique. She placed her hands on the smaller woman's hips and held her more firmly in place as the room echoed with her grunts as she drove like a battering ram into Monique.

Adrianna reached forward to grasp a handful of Monique's hair and lifted her face so she could look into the mirror and watch as her Mistress doled out her punishment. "Does it still feel good?" Adrianna asked with an almost cruel edge to her voice.

"Oh yes, Mistress," Monique said as she bit her lip to keep from crying out. Her body was in dire need to release, however Monique knew she could not until given permission by her Mistress.

"Do you want to come?"

"Yes, please, Mistress, allow me to come for you."

Adrianna's eyes glazed with the pleasure of her savage rutting and she could barely form the words she spoke next. "Come for me, Monique," she commanded and Monique cried out in blissful pleasure as Adrianna thrust deep into her and then collapsed upon her back, breathless and sated.

Adrianna could feel Monique trembling beneath her as she tried to catch her breath. She stood and removed the dildo from Monique and dropped the harness at her feet. Monique stood and took the harness into the bathroom and after cleaning the dildo, she placed it back in the drawer with the crop and harness.

Adrianna had returned to the bed, and lay back watching as Monique finished her chores and then came to kneel beside her bed. "Is there any other way I can serve you, Mistress?"

"That will be all for tonight."

"Thank you Mistress." She collected her clothing before leaving the room.

Adrianna slipped into the shower to rinse the perspiration off her body and then crept between the cool sheets and slept.

†

The following day passed quickly, and after dinner, Monique dressed Adrianna in black leather pants and button-up shirt in preparation for her evening with Marcus. When they walked into the Pit, heads turned to look at the stunning couple as they were ushered to a private table. Marcus ordered them drinks and, when they were delivered, he said a toast to her health and a long life.

"Are you ready for your birthday present?" he asked.

"You definitely have my interest. Usually you are unable to keep a secret so well hidden from me."

"It was indeed difficult, but I wanted you to be surprised by my offering."

"I am sure I will be," Adrianna watched as Marcus signaled the bartender.

A door opened at the end of the bar, and her attention was captured when a young woman walked out into the room, led by a leash attached to a leather collar around her neck. The young woman, in her twenties, was also dressed in black. She had curly dark hair that fell just below her shoulders and as she approached, Adrianna could see beautiful emerald eyes. As they approached the table, the man pulled roughly on the leash and the woman dropped to her knees before Adrianna.

"Happy birthday, my friend," Marcus said with a chuckle. "This young woman is named Celeste and she desires to become your slave if she pleases you."

43

Adrianna reached down, took the woman's chin in her hand, and lifted her face to look directly into her eyes. "Is this true?"

"Yes, Mistress, it would please me greatly to know you would have me as your slave." The woman spoke with a strong sure voice.

Adrianna could see a spark of excitement in the woman's eyes and she had the immediate perception that she would be feisty and in need of additional training. "Very well, Marcus I will accept your gift, but have the collar removed from her neck. If she proves a worthy slave, I will collar her myself.

Marcus nodded and the man removed the collar and disappeared into the crowd.

"Not a bad specimen, if I do say so myself," Marcus said as he looked at Celeste.

"She does have some beautiful traits about her, but I am sure she has much to learn before she can become a slave."

Celeste remained kneeling before Adrianna as she and Marcus shared another round of drinks.

"I am sure you are eager to take your new gift home and give her a closer inspection." Marcus stood and offered his hand to her. Celeste rose and moved back so Adrianna could stand and then followed them as they walked across the bar.

When they reached Adrianna's home, she kissed Marcus on the cheek. "Thank you for the beautiful gift."

She stepped out of the car. "Come," she ordered the woman.

Monique met them at the door and followed Adrianna into the bedroom. "Sit," Adrianna said to Celeste as she pointed to the ottoman in front of the mirror.

Monique began to undress her Mistress, carefully placing her clothing on the bed as she wrapped a soft robe around her. Adrianna sat in the oversized chair beside the bed and addressed Monique motioning toward Celeste. "Monique, this is Celeste and she desires to become my slave. The possibility of this remains to be seen, but you will assist me with her training and teach her some of the skills you have learned."

Adrianna looked Monique dead in the eyes and warned her, "You will not mistreat her and you will only touch her body when given permission, do you understand?"

"Yes, Mistress."

"Very well then, bring me my birthday present and undress her so I may see exactly what I have."

Monique walked over to Celeste, took her by the hand, and led her over to her Mistress. She unbuttoned the woman's shirt and dropped it to the floor, followed by her black lace bra. She then unfastened the young woman's jeans and slid them down her muscular legs. The woman stepped out of her loafers and then her jeans as Monique added them to the growing pile. The woman stood before Adrianna wearing only a pair of black panties. Adrianna looked at Monique and nodded her head. Monique removed the panties from Celeste.

Adrianna was pleased to see that she was cleanly shaven and her body was free of unsightly markings. "Tell me what she tastes like, Monique."

Adrianna caught a slight wince on Celeste's face at this command and her grin widened.

Celeste knew her Mistress was testing her at a critical point in her new relationship, and though she despised anyone other than her Mistress touching her, she understood her expected response. She stiffened her resolve and watched as Monique knelt before her and used her fingers to part her excited lips. Celeste felt the tip of her tongue as it encircled her opening, as Monique taunted her rival and then she sank her tongue deep inside her, licking, and swirling, as she tasted her excitement. Monique's teeth rubbed against Celeste's swollen clit and she nipped at it, giving her a sharp bite. Celeste gasped in surprise and saw the absolute glee in Monique's eyes, knowing immediately that she had made her first mistake.

Monique turned toward Adrianna. "She tastes very sweet my Mistress."

"Very good. Now I want you to tell me how well she fucks."

Monique nodded, walked over to the drawer and pulled out a red leather harness, a heavy dildo, and a tube of lubricant. As she had with her Mistress the previous evening, Monique placed the harness around Celeste's waist and attached the dildo. Instead of lubricating the dildo orally, a luxury afforded only to her Mistress, she opened the tube and spread the thick jelly over the entire length. She removed her robe, reached down, and lubricated her lips before she replaced the cap.

Monique took Celeste by the hand and led her to the mirror. She then positioned her body on all fours and instructed Celeste to move behind her. She reached between her spread legs and located the dildo, guiding it into her opening.

"Fuck her," Adrianna said as she stood and walked across the room to sit on a loveseat to allow her a better view.

46

Celeste took Monique's hips in her hands and began to move the dildo in and out of her. Adrianna watched as the muscles of her thighs and ass moved with each thrust of her body against Monique as the two women moved smoothly together. Adrianna looked into the mirror to see Celeste watching herself as she fucked Monique and she knew the woman was receiving much pleasure from the sight.

"Would you like faster, Monique?" Adrianna asked.

"Yes, please, Mistress, tell her to fuck me hard," Monique pleaded.

"You heard the woman, Celeste," Adrianna said.

Adrianna watched as Celeste began thrusting more forcefully into Monique and saw a river of perspiration run down her back as her hips slammed repeatedly into Monique's ass. She was groaning loudly and Adrianna knew she was close to orgasm. Two more minutes at this speed and Celeste's body exploded as she came hard, deep inside Monique. Monique's panting stopped as Celeste collapsed onto her back. Adrianna stood and walked to the dresser and retrieved her crop as Celeste gasped for breath.

Adrianna rained two sharp blows across Celeste's ass as she shouted, "Finish her," to the exhausted woman.

Celeste stood behind Monique and resumed driving the dildo into her body with the last remnants of her energy. When Adrianna thought Celeste was near fainting, she said, "Come Monique."

Monique cried out loudly when given permission to release by her Mistress. Celeste had made a grave mistake as she moved off Monique's body.

Monique unfastened the harness and went cleaning the dildo and was about to place it back in the drawer when Adrianna called to her. "Not so fast Monique, I want to see how good she can be fucked."

Monique smiled at her Mistress as she placed the harness around her waist and prepared the dildo. Adrianna moved back over to her chair and instructed Monique to bring her over to where she was sitting and place her on all fours. Monique did as instructed and then waited for permission to begin. Adrianna used the handle of the crop to raise Celeste's face until she looked directly into the icy-blue eyes of her Mistress.

"You will look directly at me and you will not come until I give you permission, is that understood?" she asked.

"Yes, Mistress," Celeste said.

"You may begin, Monique," Adrianna said.

"Thank you, Mistress." Monique entered Celeste with the head of the dildo and pushed until it buried inside her.

Celeste's green eyes seemed to sparkle with excitement as she locked onto Adrianna's face as instructed. The force of Monique's thrusts rocked her body back and forth and Adrianna could see her breasts sway back and forth with her movement. There was also a flame of defiance burning in those green eyes and Adrianna would teach her how to tame it without extinguishing her spirit. She could see Celeste fighting against her body's desire to release, and she was rapidly losing the battle. Low moans caught in her throat and her breathing began to quicken.

It was obvious to Adrianna that Celeste couldn't last any longer and finally surrendered to the pleasure Monique was giving her.

"Stop, Monique," Adrianna commanded harshly with disapproval evident in her voice. "Take her away from here and show her where the bathing and sleeping quarters are. Monique, you may have this weekend off, so go and visit your family."

"Yes Mistress, I will leave in the morning." Monique then helped Celeste up from the floor, and they quickly left the room.

Adrianna stretched across the bed, her anger quickly fading as she planned for the weekend of training and punishment for Celeste. The woman would have to improve dramatically if she expected to remain with her and become her slave.

†

Outside in the hall, Monique shook Celeste by the shoulders. "What on earth were you thinking in there?" she chided. "If you plan to remain here with Mistress Adrianna you will have to prove to her that you are worthy of her attention."

"I just could not hold back any longer," Celeste stammered.

Monique led her down the hallway to the bathroom. Once inside, Monique turned the water on in the tub to draw a bath and turned to look at the trembling young woman. "First lesson," she said. "When you are in the company of the Mistress the only thing you do without her permission is breathe. Mistress is a very loving and compassionate woman, but she will not tolerate a lack of discipline." Monique turned off the water and ushered Celeste into the tub.

"You must remain clean and always freshly shaven for the Mistress, and you must never issue a complaint to her regarding anything," she warned. "If she chooses to keep you, Mistress will provide very well for you and you will not lack for any material need, but you must prove to her your worthiness. "Do you understand what I am saying?" Monique asked.

"Yes, and I am thankful for your advice." Celeste began to bathe her body. "What will happen now?"

"Mistress is very displeased with your disobedience and you will undergo a weekend of training and punishment," Monique said. "How you respond to both will determine your future. If you are not up to her standards, she will dismiss you quickly, so heed my advice and warnings carefully."

"Monique, why is it that you tell me this when I can see in your eyes how much you desire the Mistress?"

"Because I, too, desired to become her slave, but we were never able to make the connection between a Master and a Slave." Disappointment was obvious in her voice as she continued. "The bond between the two goes beyond beauty and sex and the willingness to accept complete domination." They remained silent for a few minutes while Celeste finished bathing.

"So, what do I do next?" Celeste asked as she dried her body.

"You will always find clean robes in here after you bathe and you are to wear these until the Mistress decides you have earned the right to be clothed. Then she will take you out and buy the wardrobe she chooses for you to wear. Tomorrow, you and I will prepare her breakfast and then I will leave you alone with the Mistress. As instructed, I will not return until Monday."

"What kind of punishment and training should I expect?"

"Whatever the Mistress deems is necessary." Monique led Celeste down the hallway and showed her to a small bedroom where she would sleep. She returned to the bathroom to bathe before retiring for the evening.

Celeste drew back the sheets and took the robe off, laying it on a small chair beside the bed. She crept between the cool sheets and lay back as her imagination soared. She found sleep difficult because she was excited and apprehensive about the day to come. She felt she had barely drifted off to sleep when Monique knocked on her door early the next morning.

†

"Put your robe on, freshen up, and then meet me in the kitchen," Monique said.

Celeste climbed from the bed, placed the robe around her body, and made the small bed before moving to the bathroom. She washed her face, brushed her teeth and hair, and tried her best to look presentable for the Mistress. When she joined Monique in the kitchen, she learned how to prepare breakfast for the Mistress and how she enjoyed her coffee.

Monique prepared the breakfast and placed the plate and a mug of coffee on a small tray, which she handed to Celeste. She led Celeste down the hallway to the Mistress's bedroom and knocked softly on the door.

"Enter," Adrianna said.

Monique opened the door and Celeste carried the breakfast tray over to the bed and made her offering to the Mistress. Adrianna accepted the tray and laid it across her lap. She smiled at Monique. "Have a great visit with your family this weekend," Adrianna said dismissing Monique from her presence.

"You, go bathe and return when you have finished," she instructed Celeste.

After they left the room together Monique hugged Celeste. "Good luck," she wished and then left the house.

Celeste went to the bathroom and bathed quickly, not wanting to anger the Mistress any further. When she knocked on the door, Adrianna had just finished breakfast and said, "Bring me another cup of coffee, and eat some breakfast if you would like, it may be the last meal you have for a while." She handed Celeste the food tray.

Celeste returned with the coffee, went back into the kitchen to prepare and eat some toast, and then went to brush her teeth. She feared her stomach would revolt if she ate something heavier and, with a deep breath, she knocked on Adrianna's door.

†

"Come," Adrianna said from inside the room.

Celeste walked quickly across the room and knelt in front of Adrianna who had moved to the chair beside the bed. She looked up at her Mistress. "How may I serve you today, Mistress?"

"You can start by making a decision. Today you will receive punishment for your disobedience and training to teach you how to be a proper slave." Adriana looked at her closely. "Which would you like to receive first?"

"I will take my punishment first if it pleases you, Mistress." Celeste's bottom lip was quivering.

Celeste saw a slight twitch at the corner of the Mistress's mouth as she held back a smile knowing that she had chosen wisely.

"Very well then, remove your robe and follow me."

Celeste took her robe off, laid it across the ottoman, and followed Adrianna across the room. Adrianna stopped in front of the wall directly in front of the bed and instructed Celeste to stand facing the wall. Attached to the wall were four iron rings, and each held a leather restraint. Adrianna began with her arms and placed a cuff around each wrist, then securing the straps tightly through the rings. She then repeated the process with each ankle, restraining Celeste in a large X against the wall.

Adrianna walked over to the dresser and opened the top drawer, slowly withdrew a black cat-of-nine tails and closed the door. She walked back to Celeste, and touched her left ankle with the leather thongs and drew them up her leg, across her ass, and up her back.

"Cat can be your friend or foe, Celeste," Adrianna softly purred. "If you are good, Cat can bring you many pleasures," Adrianna said as she tenderly caressed the woman's bare skin with the soft leather, bringing goose flesh to the surface.

"However, if you are disobedient, Cat will bring you pain," Adrianna said as she raised her arm and brought the leather whip down across Celeste's ass. "The choice is, and always will be, yours. Last night you chose to disrespect me, and you will be punished for your behavior. Do you understand this?"

"Yes, Mistress."

"Do you know how you showed disrespect to me?"

"By not waiting for your permission, Mistress."

"Correct." Adrianna landed another blow. Small red welts were beginning to form across the smooth cheeks of her ass. Adrianna did not enjoy punishing Celeste, but she wanted to ensure she took her training and position seriously.

"A good slave will be obedient to her Mistress at all times and her needs will be met only with the permission of her Mistress, understood?" A third blow landed.

Celeste gritted her teeth against the pain she was receiving, but did not cry out. "Yes, Mistress, I understand."

"Do you understand that further disobedience will result in additional punishment?" Adrianna landed a final blow across the woman's beautiful ass.

"Yes, Mistress," Celeste panted.

Adrianna walked up behind Celeste and then stood to the side. The welts were angry, and swollen, but the skin was intact. They would leave no permanent mark on her milky skin. Adrianna looked and saw that Celeste's nipples were erect and swollen with excitement. She took the handle of the whip, and rubbed it between Celeste's spread thighs and raised it for inspection. The handle was soaked with the juices of her excitement.

"Did you enjoy that?"

"Oh yes, Mistress," Celeste answered with a soft purr in her voice.

"Good, I will be back shortly and we will begin your training."

"Thank you, Mistress."

Adrianna tossed the whip onto the bed and moved into the master bathroom. Celeste heard the sound of the shower running and her mind fantasized what it would be like to shower with the Mistress, further adding to the flow of excitement running down her spread thighs.

Adrianna showered and decided it was time to teach Celeste some control over her body. With a wicked grin on her face, she dried herself and dressed in jeans and a soft T-shirt. She applied some sensual smelling cologne, and brushed her teeth before returning to the bedroom. She left her hair wet from the shower, as she was excited to begin Celeste's training.

Adrianna stood closely behind Celeste and allowed her hands to stroke up from her hips to her firm, round breasts.

She cupped them in her hands and gave each a gentle squeeze to feel their fullness. Her nipples pressed against her palms as Adrianna softly caressed them. Adrianna stepped closer and pressed her hips into Celeste's ass as she began to gently tug at her nipples, twisting them slightly as they grew even harder under her touch. Her mouth was at Celeste's ear and she could feel the hot breath of her Mistress as she teased her body so mercilessly. She could feel Celeste's heart racing as she began speaking softly in her ear.

"You must learn to control your body to be a good slave. I will tease you and stimulate you to the point of sheer madness, but you may not come until you are given permission." Adrianna's right hand moved down between Celeste's trembling legs. She stroked her fingers over Celeste's swollen clit. "Are you ready to begin?"

"Yes Mistress," Celeste replied with a tremor in her voice.

Adrianna walked over to the drawer and opened it, pulling out a smaller dildo than the one used the previous night and walked back over to Celeste. She adjusted a wall mount to a lower level and then attached the dildo to it. She positioned it directly under the opening of Celeste's body. "Now we will work on your concentration." Adrianna opened Celeste's lips and pressed her body forward with her hips until the head of the dildo slipped inside her. Adrianna reached up to hold Celeste's wrists as she ground her hips into Celeste's body. Whispering softly again, Adrianna said, "You will continue this motion, and you will count aloud each stroke of your body onto the dildo. You will not come until I tell you. Do you understand?"

"Oh yes, Mistress," Celeste purred.

"Very good," Adrianna breathed into her ear as her fingers teased her aching nipples. Adrianna could feel

Celeste's hips brush against her, as she rocked her hips thrusting the dildo into her body. "That's it, now count."

"One, two, three," Celeste began to count with each thrust.

Adrianna stepped back and sat on the end of the bed. She watched as Celeste's ass muscles contracted with each movement.

"Ten, eleven, twelve," Celeste continued. Having to count made it much more difficult to concentrate on controlling her body, a fact Adrianna knew all too well.

"Does it feel good?"

"Yes, Mistress, sixteen, seventeen, eighteen," she breathed.

"Do you want to be fucked?"

"Oh yes, Mistress, twenty, twenty-one," Celeste moaned.

"Imagine me buried between your legs, driving into your body as my fingers are twisting your hard nipples."

Celeste cried out and her body shook with orgasm.

Adrianna stood up from her bed and picked up the whip. Without speaking, she struck a blow across her ass. "Start over," she commanded with a voice that was rough, and lacked patience. She knew she was being harsh with Celeste, but the woman showed much promise in Adrianna's eyes.

She sat back on the bed and listened as Celeste began counting again. This time Adrianna remained silent and listened to the change in Celeste's voice as she neared her peak. Then she moved behind her and pressed close, thrusting in rhythm with Celeste, as she placed her hands on Celeste's hips.

"Now you may come," Adrianna said as Celeste reached the count of thirty.

"Oh yes," Celeste cried as Adrianna's body moved with hers, and they ground roughly against the wall.

"Feel how much better that is?"

"It feels so good, Mistress."

"Rest," Adrianna said as she left the room.

Celeste allowed her body to relax as much as she could. She had worked up a sweat and could feel tiny droplets as they ran down her back and between her breasts. The welts on her ass, rubbed raw by the fabric of Adrianna's jeans and the salt stung when it reached open pores. She would not complain though, she promised herself. She heard the clock chime eleven and shortly after the Mistress returned to the room carrying a two glasses of ice water.

She heard Adrianna place what sounded like a glass on the bedside table before coming to her. The condensation trickled down the side of the glass and dripped onto her shoulder as Celeste turned her head to drink. The cold liquid felt so good to her parched throat that she did not mind the icy flow that trickled down her breasts.

When she had drunk half the glass, Adrianna turned away and walked away. "Begin."

This time Celeste was approaching forty when given permission, and she would have collapsed panting to the floor if not for the restraints. The intense response to the training her body was experiencing was incredible.

Adrianna walked over to her and remove the restraints. "Go bathe and return here."

Her body was stiff from several hours of restraint, and weak from the exertion, but Celeste gathered her robe and walked into the bathroom. She drew a bath and stepped into the luxury of the swirling water, the pain temporarily forgotten. She bathed her aching and swollen body and was amazed at how sensitive her body remained after three powerful orgasms.

She carefully dried herself, slipped a fresh robe on, and brushed her hair. When she entered the bedroom again, Adrianna looked up, "Lie down on your stomach across the bed."

Celeste did as instructed and watched as Adrianna stood up and walked to the bathroom. She returned moments later carrying a small bottle. Her hands moved under Celeste's robe and lifted it above her waist. She remained very still as Adrianna opened the bottle and poured some of the liquid into her palm. She sat the bottle on the bed and rubbed her hands together to warm the liquid, then placed her hands on Celeste's ass and tenderly caressed the soothing lotion into her irritated skin. Celeste closed her eyes and allowed herself to enjoy the gentle soothing touch of her Mistress who seemed to carefully cover each of the angry welts on her ass to soothe the pain.

When Adrianna had finished, she commanded, "Follow me to the kitchen."

†

Celeste followed Adrianna, sat at the chair she indicated, and watched as her Mistress moved gracefully around the kitchen as she prepared a sandwich and chips. Celeste was ravenous and could hardly wait to eat. Adrianna placed a plate before her. Celeste feared she was drooling since her body was starving for calories and her stomach growled its emptiness.

"Go ahead and eat."

Celeste noticed Adrianna had a faint smile on her face as she returned to prepare a sandwich for herself and pour glasses of tea for them. She watched as she carried the plate and glasses to the table and sat beside her as she was busy devouring the meal.

"Fix yourself another if you wish."

Celeste took a deep drink from the tea and stood to prepare another sandwich. "Would you care for another, Mistress?"

Adrianna chuckled. "No, I think one will be plenty for me. I will cook steaks for dinner. "Do you like steak?"

"Yes, Mistress, I do."

"We will have them for dinner." Adrianna finished her lunch.

Celeste continued to eat watching as Adrianna placed the steaks in marinate and prepared potatoes for baking.

"After you finish your meal, you will retire to your room to rest awhile. When you wake, you may prepare a salad for us and place it in the refrigerator to chill. After dinner, your training will continue," Adrianna said before leaving the kitchen to return to her bedroom for a nap.

Adrianna had difficulty falling asleep. Her imagination soared as she planned the remainder of Celeste's training. She was impressed by how well the young woman had accepted her punishment and how quickly she responded to her training. Her skills demonstrated tonight would determine if she had a future with Adrianna. Smiling to herself, Adrianna's mind and body relaxed and she drifted into a peaceful sleep.

After Adrianna left, Celeste quickly picked up the kitchen and went to her room to rest as the Mistress had instructed. She removed her robe and lay face down on the bed, the soft sheet barely grazing the inflamed skin covering her ass. The lotion that the Mistress had placed on the welts had relieved most of the pain and swelling, but some movements painfully reminded Celeste that she had received her punishment. Thinking of how the leather felt on her skin made Celeste shiver with expectation of more training. The memory of the Mistress grinding her body into hers as she came and the scent of her cologne made her nipples throb with ache, and she prayed that Mistress would take her tonight. She closed her eyes and willed her body to sleep.

Two hours later, she awoke, prepared a salad for their dinner, placed it in the refrigerator to chill, and placed the potatoes in the oven.

†

Celeste crept quietly into the Mistress's bedroom and knelt beside the bed. The Mistress was sleeping so peacefully and Celeste took advantage of the opportunity to examine her Mistress more closely. She watched the sheet rise and fall across her chest as Adrianna breathed slowly in her sleep and her mouth twitch, as she was deep in her dreams. One of her legs had moved from beneath the covers and Celeste admired the long, smooth muscles of her tanned body. Celeste could feel her body growing wet and she fought off the desire to reach between her legs and stroke herself as she fantasized about the Mistress. Instead, she sat back on her heels and waited for the mistress to awaken.

A short while later Adrianna began to stir. Celeste was still kneeling beside the bed when her Mistress awoke and gave her a slight smile. "Join me upon the bed." Celeste stood and walked around the side of the bed and sat upon it.

"Lie back and get comfortable"

Celeste stretched her body across the bed and waited for her next command. She hoped that the Mistress would desire to give her body pleasure, but this was not yet to be.

"Show me how you please yourself." Adrianna turned on her side.

Celeste had never masturbated in front of another before and her cheeks flushed slightly with embarrassment.

"You have never done this before, have you?" Adrianna asked.

"No, Mistress, not in front of anyone."

"Good, this will be a first for you. Begin."

Celeste spread her legs slightly as she began running her hands over her body. She laid her head back against a pillow and closed her eyes as her body came alive with arousal. Adrianna watched as Celeste's fingers began to tease her nipples, circling them slowly with her fingers, as they grew to chiseled peaks, the small blood vessels surrounding them swelling as they delivered blood to the sensitive flesh. Her breathing changed when she began pinching them as her body started to writhe under her touch. Celeste's right hand caressed its way down her body and came to rest above her mound. She placed the soles of her feet together and bent her legs opening her thighs and the lips of her womanhood spread to reveal delicate pink ridges.

Celeste's tongue licked her lips as the tips of her fingers brushed across her exposed clit and her hips began to undulate on the bed. Her juices quickly coated her fingers as she stroked her clit, her left hand moving down to spread her lips open. Celeste's fingers caressed both sides of her opening. Adrianna watched as she struggled to hold back her moans of pleasure.

"You can enjoy your pleasure." Adrianna gave her permission to make any sound she desired. She watched as Celeste's fingers slowly entered her body as she moaned with intense pleasure. She began with one and progressed to three fingers moving deeply in and out, moving slowly as her thumb stroked across her clit. Adrianna's hunger grew as Celeste's arousal soared. She could smell the musky scent of her and watched as the juices flowed from her with each stroke. Celeste's stomach muscles began to contract and Adrianna knew the young woman was close to her climax. She looked into her face to find Celeste's emerald eyes fixed on her as they begged for release.

"Let it go," Adrianna said and Celeste's body exploded as her orgasm seemed to rip through every inch of her. Her fingers continued to plunge deep until her pleasure began to subside and she slowly withdrew her fingers and looked into Adrianna's eyes.

Adrianna smiled at her for the first time. "Very beautiful."

"Take a shower while I start the steaks and when you have finished, you may prepare the table for dinner. You will find a bottle of Pinot Noir on the counter rack, pour us a glass, and join me on the pool deck until the steaks are done." She dressed in her jeans and soft T-shirt. She started to leave the room and stopped to turn back toward the bed. "How do you like your steak cooked?"

"Medium rare if that pleases you, Mistress."

"Good, I will see you soon." She left the room.

Celeste remained on the Mistress's bed a few more moments and she dared to reach over and bring the pillow Adrianna had slept on to her face. She breathed deeply taking in a lungful of the rich fragrance she wore and she hoped to smell more of it later. With a deep sigh, she left the bed and quickly showered.

†

Adrianna walked out to the pool and turned on the grill. She sat on a chaise lounge and watched as the sun dipped below the horizon and the night began to fall. When the grill was ready, she walked back into the house to retrieve the steaks and heard the shower turn off in the bathroom. She smiled to herself as she stepped back onto the deck and placed the steaks on the grill. She was pleased with Celeste so far, and tonight would be the final test to see if she was a potential for further training.

Through the door she watched as Celeste came into the kitchen and prepared the table before pouring them each a glass of the fragrant wine she had set out. Celeste carried the glasses out to the pool deck closing the door behind her. When she handed her the glass of wine, desire burned in Adrianna making her pulse jump.

"Thank you." Adrianna's voice was soft and pleasant. "Sit with me. Tell me about yourself."

"I am a part-time legal assistant with a law firm in town and I am a law student at the University in the afternoons."

"What type of law do you want to pursue?"

"I hope to specialize in corporate law. I have completed my first three years of study and hope to finish in the next four to prepare for the bar examination."

"I imagine it is difficult to study and work part time."

"I have managed so far. I need to work to pay tuition and rent on my small apartment."

Adrianna stood and walked to the grill to check the steaks. *It would certainly be easier for Celeste to focus on school full time if she lived here. She would have no need to work.* She turned the steaks.

She walked back to take her seat. "Why do you wish to be my slave?"

Celeste blushed at the question. "I find you incredibly attractive and I know that if I give myself to you completely, you will show me a love like no other."

Intelligent and confident. Adrianna looked at the blushing woman. "Are you willing to follow my every command without hesitation?"

"Yes, Mistress, but with one exception, if I may ask."

Adrianna raised a brow. "Which would be what?"

"I only ask that you not force me to be used by a man," Celeste said boldly.

Adrianna stood and walked back to raise the lid on the grill to mask the grin playing on her face. She would never ask Celeste to perform that task, preferring instead to keep her for her own desires, with maybe an occasional performance with another female slave or Mistress, just to keep her humble.

Adrianna turned and walked back to Celeste and took her chin in her hands raising her eyes to meet hers. "I can work with that exception, if that is all you ask."

"That is all, Mistress."

Adrianna rewarded her with another of her brilliant smiles. "The steaks will be done in just a moment. Go bring me a platter for them, take the potatoes out of the oven, and fill them with butter."

Adrianna walked into the kitchen, placed a thick steak on each plate, and rinsed the platter in the sink before returning to the table. Celeste, who had brought the chilled salads to the table, joined her. "During meals you may speak freely."

"Thank you, Mistress." Celeste poured dressing on her salad. "Would you care for more wine, Mistress?"

"Yes, please."

Celeste poured them another glass of the wine; they enjoyed the meal and spoke often while they ate. Adrianna was becoming more impressed with each new item of information she learned from Celeste. When the meal was done and Celeste had cleared the table, Adrianna said, "Pour us another glass of wine and follow me."

Celeste poured the contents of the bottle into the two glasses and carried them as she followed Adrianna into the bedroom.

Adrianna took a glass from Celeste and gently touched the two glasses together. "To your training," she raised the glass to her lips and drank.

Celeste also took a deep drink and handed the glass to her Mistress. Adrianna placed the glasses on the bedside table and turned back to Celeste.

"I want you to draw a bath for me and then bathe me. I like the water very warm and candles lit around the tub. You will also find a bottle of lotion on the counter. You will use to cover my skin after you have dried me."

"Yes, Mistress."

Celeste left to prepare the bath. When she returned she said, "The water is ready, the candles are lit, and made sure I know where the lotion is. I've set out a thick, soft towel and a fresh robe for you, Mistress.

Adrianna stood and Celeste removed her shirt, and then knelt to remove the jeans from her Mistress. She took the clothes, placed them in a hamper, and followed her Mistress into the bathroom.

Adrianna stepped into the bath as Celeste turned off the lights as instructed. Adrianna lowered her head and wet her hair as her body soaked in the warm water.

Celeste picked up a bottle of shampoo and washed her hair, rinsing the rich lather with a small vase sitting on the tub's edge. She picked up a soft sponge and lathered it with liquid soap as she began to bathe her Mistress. She washed every part of her body with tender care and rinsed her carefully. Adrianna laid her head back on the pillow and relaxed for a few minutes while Celeste continued to kneel next to her, watching as the shadows from the candle flame flickered across her Mistress's face.

When Adrianna opened the drain, Celeste stood and opened the oversized towel, wrapping Adrianna's body with it as she patted her dry. Adrianna sat on the edge of the tub while Celeste brushed her hair then began caressing the smooth lotion into her skin.

Adrianna stood and allowed Celeste to place a robe around her. She took Celeste in her arms and lifted her face. She bent her head down and her soft lips met no resistance as they shared their first kiss. The sweet wine remained on both their tongues as they swirled slowly while they explored each other's mouths. Adrianna's hands moved to untie the sash around Celeste's waist and lowered the robe as they kissed.

Her hands stroked down Celeste's back and she cupped her ass in her hands giving each cheek a firm squeeze before moving up her body. The kiss deepened and, as her hands moved between their bodies, she covered Celeste's breasts with her soft hands. She could feel the nipples growing hard against her palm and she gently kneaded her breasts.

Adrianna backed the smaller woman against the vanity and broke the kiss long enough to lift her on the vanity, making them equal in height. She covered Celeste's mouth with hers again as her hands returned to caress and tease

Celeste's breasts, pinching her nipples as she kissed her deeply. Adrianna's body was on fire and she reached down to unfasten her robe, allowing it to fall open. She took Celeste's right hand and placed it between her thighs so she could feel how excited she was and felt the moan she released into Adrianna's mouth.

Adrianna removed her hand and broke the kiss. She took Celeste by the hand and led her to the bed, placing her on her back as she climbed onto the bed and lowered herself onto Celeste. Adrianna's hips forced Celeste's thighs wide as she covered her mouth with a sweltering kiss. Celeste wrapped her legs around the back of Adrianna's thighs and began grinding into her Mistress. Adrianna could feel the woman's dampness, and her mouth moved to Celeste's neck, licking down to the dip between her neck and shoulder, nipping at the sensitive skin as her fingers twisted Celeste's throbbing nipples.

Adrianna moved further down the bed until her mouth was directly above Celeste's left nipple. The tip of her tongue flicked across her nipple and slowly circled each before she lowered her mouth to take her entire breast in her mouth, sucking it deeply as her hand kneaded and teased the other.

The movement of Celeste's hips quickened as Adrianna's mouth drove her wild with need. She prayed that her Mistress would move further down to give her body pleasure, but Adrianna had a different plan.

Adrianna easily rolled her body, taking Celeste with her and guided her mouth down to cover her right breast. Celeste was delighted to be able to serve her Mistress and eagerly sucked her breast, nibbling at her swollen nipples and sucking roughly as Adrianna's hand guided her more firmly onto her breast. She then bent her knees and raised them until her feet lay flat on the bed, with Celeste's lower body snuggled into her wetness. Adrianna placed her hands on top of Celeste's head and guided her down her body. Celeste licked and kissed her way down her Mistress, eager to finally taste her sweetness. When she lay between her legs, Celeste used the tips of her fingers to gently part Adrianna's lips as she lowered her face onto her mound. Her tongue lapped at the sweet liquid welled between her lips, and she moaned at the exquisite taste of her Mistress.

Her tongue slipped between the soaked lips, and she explored the depths of Adrianna as her tongue probed and licked her Mistress while her fingers brushed across her throbbing clit. The movement and speed of Celeste's tongue slowly brought Adrianna to the edge of orgasm, and she began to feel the quaking of her body as her Mistress climaxed, her body shaking with violent spasms as she soaked Celeste's face with her juices.

After Adrianna climaxed, she relaxed on the bed while Celeste continued to lick softly, enjoying the taste of her pleasure. Adrianna sat up and laid Celeste on her back with her head at the foot of the bed. She placed a small pillow under her head and propped it against the wooden rail of the footboard. Adrianna then bent Celeste's knees, spread her thighs, and instructed Celeste to hold the backs of her knees to keep her legs spread. Celeste hooked her hands behind her knees and watched as Adrianna's mouth moved down to cover her mound. Celeste feared she would faint as Adrianna's tongue slid deeply inside her and she bit her tongue to keep from crying out in pleasure.

Adrianna licked and probed inside Celeste and then raised her mouth to cover Celeste's clit as two long fingers replaced her tongue deep inside her. Her lips tugged at her clit while her fingers plunged in and out of her as she thrust deep and hard. Adrianna could feel Celeste's inner muscles contracting around her fingers as she neared orgasm.

"Come for me, Celeste," she covered her clit with a fiery kiss. Celeste's body thrashed beneath Adrianna as her orgasm crashed over her body and mind as she cried out in blissful pleasure.

Celeste's eyes still burned with passion, and she dared to speak. "Fuck me please, Mistress."

Adrianna left the bed and walked to the dresser. She opened the drawer and pulled out the leather harness, fastening it around her waist and then placed the dildo on the mount. She reached inside the drawer and picked up two small items she left concealed in her hand. She walked back to the bed and sat Celeste on its edge. She leaned down and let the fingers of her right-hand twist Celeste's nipples and they filled with blood as they quickly swelled.

Adrianna opened her left hand to reveal two nipple clamps with leaded weights at their ends. She placed one around each nipple tightly, and then gave each one a gentle tug to insure they were securely in place. Celeste bit down on her lower lip to keep from crying out as her nipples continued to swell.

Adrianna offered her a hand and led her over to the mirror. Celeste knelt on all fours, her breasts dangling off the front of the ottoman, the weights keeping constant pressure on her throbbing nipples. Adrianna pressed the length of the dildo between Celeste's thighs and coated its length with her juices as she rocked her hips back and forth. Celeste reached between her legs, positioned the head of the dildo against her opening, and waited for her Mistress to begin.

Adrianna placed her hands on Celeste's hips and began to slowly stroke into her, rocking her gently as the clamps tightened further on her nipples. Celeste's body pulsed with arousal as her Mistress took her slowly and the agonizing pleasure her nipples were experiencing made silence nearly impossible. She looked up into the mirror and locked eyes with her Mistress. There was complete ecstasy in the icy-blue eyes that were looking through her to her soul as she took Celeste's body for her own, stroking deeper and harder as their bodies began to rock in rhythm to the cries of their pleasure. Both women were coated with perspiration as they forced their bodies under control until they reached the apex of their passion.

"Come with me, Celeste," Adrianna cried out. With a final brutal thrust of her hips, she shuddered with violent spasms as her orgasm tore its way from her body. Celeste thrashed beneath Adrianna as she climaxed again and again until she blacked out.

Adrianna withdrew from her slowly and removed the harness as she staggered to her oversized chair and collapsed. Her legs trembled from exertion, her heart raced wildly in her chest, and she struggled to control her breathing. She had just felt the most intense orgasm of her life and the feeling both comforted her and overwhelmed her. Her body was soaked and her fever grew hotter as she watched Celeste stand and walk toward her. She stopped before her Mistress and dropped to her knees.

Adrianna reached out and removed the clamps from her raw and swollen nipples, laying them on the table. She raised Celeste to her feet and led her from the bedroom and out to the pool. She guided them down the steps and into the cooling waters, forcing them under the surface to dowse their heated bodies. When they surfaced, Adrianna embraced Celeste and kissed her softly as she walked her backward through the water to the pool steps. She pressed Celeste onto the top step and placed her body between Celeste's trembling legs. Their tongues swirled together, each tasting a mixture of wine and the essence of their shared pleasure.

Adrianna broke the kiss and leaned down to take each nipple gently into her mouth and she kissed them sweetly.

She placed her arms underneath Celeste's knees and raised her body until her wetness was inches from Adrianna's mouth. She parted her lips with gentle fingertips, and her tongue began to caress Celeste's lips, slipping between them to drink from her well of desire as she groaned her pleasure.

"Come for me, darling," she instructed. Adrianna's tongue stroked and probed inside her until Celeste again shook with the extreme pleasure her Mistress gave her. She continued to lick until Celeste collapsed in exhaustion and Adrianna picked up her small body and carried her to the chaise lounge where she wrapped her arms around her protectively. Adrianna smiled as she realized Marcus had indeed given her the perfect gift. She nuzzled into Celeste's neck and together they sank into an exhausted sleep.

The Window Seat

It was late Friday afternoon when my flight finally arrived in Memphis. I was concerned that I would not arrive on time to make my connecting flight to the Twin Cities, but the weather that had delayed my arrival also had planes grounded in Memphis. I was tired from a long week, but had chosen to fly half the route from Florida to Salt Lake with a weekend layover in the Twin Cities. I had intentionally planned the trip this way to do some shopping and to break up the long flight.

I made the departure gate and found the waiting area swarming with impatient travelers. My flight had been delayed an hour and a half so I wandered inside the closest bar for a drink. The waitress brought me an icy beer as I settled onto the hard barstool. I took a pull from the bottle and looked up at one of the multitude of TVs in the bar to find a college softball game underway. At least I would have an enjoyable way of killing time I thought as I sipped my beer.

I glanced into the mirror behind the bar and noticed a woman sitting at a table near the middle of the bar, and she was looking in my direction. Probably just watching the game too I thought, as I smiled at her and was rewarded with a smile that lit the room in return. Her jet-black hair was curly, cascading below her shoulders, and her eyes looked as dark as coal when they locked onto mine in the mirror. I felt my cheeks flush as I admired how beautiful she was and my eyes lingered on her image in the mirror. The waitress stopped by to ask if I needed anything and I ordered another beer. When I looked back up into the mirror, the beautiful dark-haired woman was gone.

The overhead intercom called a flight for Knoxville, and the large man on my right that I had been bumping elbows with, got up from his barstool and staggered out of the bar. I scooted my stool a little more to the right to give me additional room and continued sipping on my beer. My heart skipped a beat when a silky smooth voice from behind me asked, "Pardon me, but is this seat taken?" I turned on my stool to see the dark-haired stranger there, gesturing toward the stool vacant to my right.

"No ma'am, please, be my guest," I offered with a smile.

"Thanks, my name is Maria." She extended her hand.

I took her soft hand gently into mine. "You're welcome, and my name is Court."

"Nice to meet you, Court." She gently squeezed my hand. "May I buy you another beer?"

I looked at my watch and saw that I still had another hour before my flight. "Sure, that would be nice."

Maria ordered a white wine and another beer from the waitress. "Where are you bound?"

"Salt Lake City eventually, but I am laying over in the Twin Cities for the weekend. How about you?"

"I'm heading home to St. Paul. Looks like we both have the same wait," she added with that heart-stopping smile. "You like college softball?"

"I love watching it. I never had a chance to play fast pitch, so the game intrigues me."

"Well from the looks of you, I bet you're still in good enough shape to give it a try," Maria noted, with a wicked gleam in her eyes.

"I doubt I could catch up to one of those pitches to hit it," I said. "My hands move a little slower these days."

Maria arched an eyebrow. "Slow hands can be very good."

I nearly fell off my chair as this beautiful woman flirted with me. This layover might pass more quickly than I wished I thought as I looked into the dark eyes that were focused on me. I watched as she raised the wine glass to her lips and tilted her head back revealing a long, slender neck. I could see the pulse-throbbing vein. This woman had an aura of pure sensuality around her, and obviously knew the effect she was having on me as my tongue encircled my lips, wetting them as I watched her movements, my mouth aching to caress her neck, my tongue yearning to feel the throbbing pulse.

"Where are you staying in the Cities?" Maria asked.

"I thought I would get a room close to the airport when I arrive."

"That will not do," Maria chuckled. "Please allow me to make a few arrangements for you. My husband and I own several nice resort properties there and I will not take no for an answer. You are obviously a road-worn traveler, past due for some relaxation, and I know just the place."

Damn, a husband, I thought as I listened to her. I did not see a wedding ring on her hand so I had made a false assumption. Figures though that a woman this beautiful could not possibly be single for long.

I watched as she reached into her bag and took out a smartphone. With a swipe and a touch, she was connected and made arrangements to have me placed in a suite. I was speechless as I listened to her order up the VIP package and transportation from the airport. I was barely able to whisper, "Lewis," as she confirmed the reservation in my name. She put the phone back in her bag and gave me one of her alluring smiles. "You're all booked."

I regained enough composure to thank her.

With another of her blinding smiles, she said, "It is my pleasure and my treat. I hope when you return to our city you will use our services again."

To say that I was in overwhelmed would have been an understatement and I was searching my brain for a comment to relay my appreciation when she put a finger to my lips and said, "Listen, I do believe that is our call."

We stood, gathering our belongings, left a generous tip for our waitress, and walked toward our gate. I pulled out my ticket to find that I'd been upgraded to First Class and my heart pounded with the thought of spending another two hours seated beside this beautiful creature. I smiled as we compared seat assignments. Lady luck was indeed smiling down on me when we discovered our seats were together.

"Looks like you are stuck with me a little while longer," I teased.

"You are much nicer looking than most of the others in First Class," she whispered as we looked around at the crowd of mostly older businessmen surrounding us. I laughed and, with a wink, we headed down the ramp to our seats. We stowed our bags in the overhead compartment and took our seats settling in while the other passengers boarded. We talked about careers and she shared with me that she traveled extensively to monitor the numerous properties they owned, and searched for new properties to purchase. She had been down in Memphis looking at a few prospects this week. I told her that I was in Health Care Management and was going out to Salt Lake to look at several properties my company was interested in acquiring.

The attendant brought us both a glass of wine while we were waiting to take flight, and we sipped the smooth wine and continued to talk. The drink had a very calming effect on me and shortly after we departed, I felt my eyes growing heavy.

Maria leaned over to me, "Will you get my laptop down for me, so I will not have to disturb your nap?"

"Certainly," I answered, suddenly eager to please this woman in any way that I could. I rose and removed the laptop from the case and handed her the small computer, and then located a pillow and blanket for myself. "Flight time is usually the best sleep I get all week," I admitted, "but feel free to punch me if I start snoring."

"Oh, I will," she promised. She opened the laptop and I snuggled under my blanket for a short nap. I drifted off to sleep listening to the soft tapping of the keys, as she worked on some unknown project.

A slight turbulence caused the jet to bounce. I awoke to find my head resting on Maria's shoulder and my left hand draped comfortably across her waist. Slightly embarrassed, I stumbled through an apology. Maria said that she had enjoyed the closeness, and she hoped I would continue resting there. Unwilling to deny my benefactor such pleasurable hospitality, I again rested my head on her shoulder. She nuzzled her cheek against the top of my head and closed the file she was working on and opened a new one.

The heat from her body caressed my hand as it rested on her waist and my fingers twitched with desire to touch her. I watched in silence as she began to type onto the small screen.

I am enjoying the feel of your head resting on my shoulder, and the twitching of your fingers on my waist has me hoping that they are wishing to touch me further. If I am correct, spread your blanket over your shoulder and allow it to drop into my lap.

She obviously knew I would be able to read the screen from this position as she typed and I eagerly responded to her words, spreading the soft blanket across her lap.

Maria continued to type. *Slide your hand down my thigh until you can feel the soft skin that is burning for your touch.*

My fingers trembled slightly as my hand moved down across her hip and onto her silk covered thigh. I had not realized until then that Maria was wearing a skirt and was elated that after a short descent, my hand touched smooth, naked skin. My heart was racing as I slowly caressed the soft skin on her firm thigh.

That feels really nice. If you are interested, feel free to explore. As she typed, she spread her legs in invitation.

My hand worked its way underneath the silky fabric and I slowly started to caress the inside of her thigh. I looked down her body to see her erect nipples pressing hard against the silky blouse. It was obvious she was taking pleasure from my touch. As I stroked my fingertips across her thigh, I saw her heart pounding in the pulse of her neck. I raised my mouth to her ear, "I want you so very much, Maria." She responded with a muffled moan, took her hand and placed it on top of mine, guiding me farther up her body.

I was not surprised when I reached her center to find that she was not wearing any panties. However, I was surprised to find that she was smoothly shaven. It was my turn to moan as my fingers brushed across her bare lips.

"I would love to have my mouth right here," I whispered as my fingers traveled down her wet lips. "Let my tongue slide down inside you and drink from you for hours." I could feel her body begin to quiver as my voice continued to seduce and my fingers teased.

The lights in the cabin were turned off to allow travelers to sleep and Maria's hand reached up to turn the overhead off that she had been using, leaving our seats in concealing darkness. I took the lobe of her ear in my mouth, sucking softly on it, and then whispered, "This is what I'd like to do to your clit." I sucked her lobe deeply in and out of my mouth.

Maria's hand pressed on top of mine as she urged me onward and I let my fingertips gently part her lips and stroke down the sides of her opening, drawing moisture up and across her throbbing clit. Her hand covered mine as my thumb stroked across her clit and our fingers entwined as our middle two fingers entered her, pressing deep into her wetness. Maria let out a gasp as our fingers rubbed lightly against her G spot and her body began to vibrate with excitement. With her free hand, she guided my face to hers and our lips met in a soft, tender kiss. I could feel her hips rocking into our hands as her lips parted and she pulled my tongue deeply into her mouth for a hungry kiss. I felt her juices rush past our fingers as her body erupted in orgasm and her tongue went wild inside my mouth, her moans muffled by the deep kiss.

Still kissing, I slowly withdrew our fingers and I could feel her climax continue as she moaned deeply in my mouth. I raised our hands, taking both of our fingers into my mouth to suck the moisture from them, licking slowly, and savoring every drop of the sweet nectar. I kissed her deeply so she could taste her sweetness as it filled my mouth, our tongues dancing slowly together.

We could feel the jet as it started to descend and Maria powered off her laptop and handed it back to me. I returned it to the overhead and sat beside her. My hand rested on the armrest between us as the cabin slowly came back to life, and she reached over to cover my hand with hers.

As we touched down and began to taxi to the terminal she again pulled out her cell telephone and powered it on. She dialed her husband and quickly told him that something had come up and she would be home later in the weekend. With a quick farewell, she closed the telephone and turned it back off. I looked at her with a curious smile and she asked, "Mind if I am your personal guide to the Cities this weekend?"

"I would love that." I squeezed her hand. "I bet you know all the local hotspots."

"Not sure about that, but I know one I am going to get into real soon," her hand disappeared beneath the blanket and she cupped my mound.

†

We retrieved our luggage and located the driver who greeted Maria. "Hello, Mrs. Santos, how are you doing this evening?"

"Tired Carlos. Carlos, this is Ms. Lewis and she will be staying with us this weekend. Make sure she gets anywhere she wants to go while she's here."

"Will do Mrs. Santos, and Ms. Lewis, it is my pleasure to serve you." He opened the door to a sleek black limo and took our bags for storage.

The lights of the city greeted us as we left the airport and headed downtown. Maria snuggled in close to me as we rode through the city, her hand stroking up and down my thigh as she pointed out highlights of the city. My concentration was torn, between listening to her soft voice and the movements of her hand stimulating my body. I was on fire for her, and she knew it, as her mouth kissed up my neck while she moved to straddle my lap.

My fingers slid easily inside her, as her body lowered to grind into my lap and onto my probing fingers. Her lips on my neck were relentless and her hips rocked harder into my body as we wound through the city. Maria cried out, "I am coming, baby," as she bit into my shoulder. Her hands covered my breasts as she continued to slowly rock back and forth on my fingers, my nipples rolled between her fingers as we slowly pulled up to our destination. With a kiss that promised a night of pleasure, she moved from my lap, straightening her clothes just as Carlos came around to open the door for us.

A bellman carried our bags up to the room as Maria stopped at the front desk to check for messages. In minutes, we were inside a huge suite, filled with every imaginable amenity. The hot tub was bubbling, an open bottle of champagne and two glasses sat waiting for us on the edge of the tub. Maria moved about the room, lighting candles and dimming the lights in the bedroom. Her fingers pressed buttons on a remote and soft music began playing, a pulsing beat vibrating throughout the room.

She walked over to stand in front of me and began to slowly remove my clothing. She unbuttoned my shirt, carefully tossing it onto a small chair, while her fingers deftly worked the fasteners on my bra. Her mouth covered a breast, as her hands busily worked the fasteners on my slacks, sliding them down my hips, and off with ease. My fingers slid the zipper of her skirt down and she kicked it off toward the growing pile of clothes. My hand slid beneath her blouse, and with one fluid movement, her blouse, and bra slipped over her head. Then I felt her hands guide my panties to the floor.

She took my hand and led me to the hot tub, handing me a glass of the champagne as I settled back into the swirling water. She sipped the champagne as she waded across the tub toward me, her luscious breasts floating across the water. When she stood before me, she knelt on the ledge straddling my waist, while raising her upper body completely out of the water. Her breasts were inches from my face as she slowly poured the remaining champagne in the glass down the front of her body. I leaned forward to catch the small river of bubbles as it ran down her left breast and licked my way up to her nipple. My hands encircled her back as I pulled her into my mouth and began suckling her gently at first, and then with a growing need. Her nails were dragging up and down my back as my teeth nibbled her sensitive nipples. Maria moaned loudly her pleasure and she raised to a standing position on the ledge, placing her hands against the wall for support. I placed my hands on her hips and pulled her forward, my fingertips spreading her lips to expose Maria's throbbing clit. I moved the tip of my tongue in small circles around it as her moans echoed in the room.

My ears picked up the beat of the music, and I took Maria's clit in my mouth and started to suck it in and out of my mouth. My mouth matched the slow pulsing beat as three of my fingers entered her, burying themselves in her velvety wetness. My mouth worked on her clit, my teeth rubbing against it as my fingers began plunging in and out of her body. Maria's hand slid down from the wall to bury itself in my hair as she ground my mouth onto her clit. My teeth surrounded her clit as she said, "Oh yes, baby, I am coming!" and she collapsed against the wall for support. She reached between her legs and slowly withdrew my fingers raising them to her mouth. She sucked them gently clean and then she stood in front of me and pulled me to my feet.

"Now, I get to have you." She smiled wickedly.

She helped me from the hot tub, patted me dry with a soft towel, and then led me to the large bed, laying me down on my back. She quickly dried and lay down beside me, her right thigh draped over mine. I could feel the moisture on my thigh as she moved up my body to kiss me. Her tongue explored every inch of my mouth as her fingers twisted my nipples and her knee pressed between my thighs.

I pulled her on top of me as we kissed, her bare mound pressing into me as I used my hands to pull her up and down my body, our nether lips joining and her hot clit pressing onto mine. She thrashed as we came together, our bodies moving in unison as we rode the waves of pleasure.

Her mouth traveled down my skin until she was nestled between my thighs, her hot tongue probing deeply inside me. Maria's elbows hooked under my knees, spreading me open, as her fingers rubbed furiously across the top of my clit bringing me close. I pushed a small pillow under my hips and reached down to stop her movements long enough to guide her body on top of mine in a sixty-nine position, her cleanly shaven lips a mere inch from my face as she lowered her head back between my thighs. My fingers parted her lips and my tongue entered her deeply, matching her stroke for stroke. My thumb found her clit waiting for attention and as I stroked it, she began to rock on my face.

I bent my legs to raise my knees and began pushing my hips up into her face, driving her tongue deeper into me as I moved my face from side to side, my tongue buried in her vagina. I could feel Maria start to come on top of me, sending me tumbling over the edge, as I reached down to pull her mouth up to my clit and I joined her in a dance of orgasm. Our bodies convulsed with pleasure as our faces were coated with one another's juices. Maria rolled off me, and turned to face me, a look of desire still in her eyes.

"I need one more, Court," Maria said. "You up for it?"

My smile answered her question as I leaned toward her. She stopped me with her hand and said, "Just a second," as she slipped off the bed. Maria went to her luggage and pulled out a large vibrating dildo. Crawling onto the bed she said, "I want you to use this," as she handed me the dildo and rolled over on her belly.

She rose to her knees, spreading her legs wide and I twisted the top of the dildo turning the vibrator on, feeling it jump to life in my hand. I sat up on the bed beside her and slowly started moving the dildo across her lips, coating it with her juices as the vibrations kissed her most sensitive spots.

"Umm, feels so good Court," Maria purred, her hips rocking to the beat of the music. After several minutes of stroking, Maria reached down between her legs and spread her lips. "Just listen to the beat, Court," Maria said as she reached for the remote to turn up the volume.

I placed the head of the dildo at Maria's opening and slowly entered her, the dildo spreading her lips wide. Once more, my ears tuned into the beat of the music, and I began to move slowly in and out of Maria, inch after inch disappearing into her aroused body. The beat of the music was rapidly increasing and following Maria's orders; my hips increased speed, driving deep inside her with each stroke. Maria started to growl as I stroked faster and faster, maintaining a frantic pace. I reached underneath her, rubbing my palm against her clit, which sent her tumbling out of control. She came so violently I was afraid she would hurt herself. She placed her hand on my wrist, pushing the dildo out of her depths and fell face forward on the bed. I twisted off the vibrator and tossed it to the end of the bed as I lay down next to her. I reached down to the end of the bed and pulled the covers over our exhausted bodies and took Maria in my arms as we drifted off to sleep.

The next morning, I awoke to an empty bed. On the nightstand sat a single yellow rose, and a note, which read:

> *My Darling Court,*
> *Thanks for a beautiful night. I have a few errands to run this morning, and I did not want to wake you. I will be back about lunchtime to take you on a tour of the city as promised. Call Room Service and order a hearty breakfast. You are going to need the energy.*
> *By the way, I left a present for you. All you have to do is push play. See you for lunch!*
> *Maria*

I sat back against the headboard of the bed and reached for the remote. I pushed play and a video popped up on the screen, which started from when we entered the room. I pushed pause and ordered breakfast, then watched the entire video, which left me hungry for more than food. I showered, dressed, and waited for Maria's return.

What a trip this had turned out to be I thought as I lay on the couch. Maybe I should plan to visit the Twin Cities more often.

I was deep in thought when Maria returned, the snap of the electronic key the only sound of her entrance. She walked into the room carrying several bags, which she sat on a chair. As she approached, I moved to sit up on the couch, but her hand easily held me in place as she lowered herself onto me. The warmth of her body burned into my skin as her mouth covered mine with a passionate kiss.

My hands instinctively moved down to her hips and she began to slowly grind into me, as our kiss grew more heated. Entwined, we both approached our peak of passion when Maria suddenly stopped her movements and broke the kiss. "I want you hungry tonight, lover. I bought a new toy that I can't wait for you to use when we return." Maria leaned down to kiss me again and said, "But now, we are off to see the city."

Maria rose from the couch and extended her hand to me and together we walked to the elevator. When we reached the front door of the lobby, Carlos was there, waiting with the limo. "Hello, Carlos," I said.

"Good afternoon, Ms. Lewis, I hope you are having a pleasant stay with us."

"Yes, I am, Carlos, very much so," I said as he opened the door for us.

"To the Riverside Park," Maria said to him as I stepped into the back seat.

"Yes, Mrs. Santos." He closed the door behind us.

Maria pointed out a variety of different points of interest as we again wound our way through the city. A new cultural center had just opened the previous week and Maria promised we would stop in later to tour the exhibits of local artists on display there. I could sense the excitement in her voice as we neared the park and she pointed out several hot air balloons that were floating high above.

"Those are beautiful." I marveled at the colorful balloons that rose high into the air above the city. "That must be a fabulous view." I turned to look at Maria, to find her eyes were sparkling with excitement.

"In just a few minutes you can tell me how fabulous the view is."

"What?"

"We are going for a hot air balloon ride."

"That is fantastic!" I watched the joy on her face continue to glow.

Carlos pulled the limo into an open field and walked around to open the door for us. "Have a good time, ladies, and I will be back for you in an hour." He closed the door behind us.

"Thank you, Carlos." Maria took my hand and we walked over to a waiting balloon.

Maria paid the gentleman for the ride and he gave us a brief explanation of how the balloon worked. The balloon was completely tethered, would float high enough to give the passengers a three hundred-sixty-degree view of the Twin Cities and the surrounding countryside. The tether would slowly draw the balloon around a circuit the size of two football fields to give the riders a complete panoramic view and the ride would last just over an hour. The man opened the door to the open basket and secured it behind us. "Enjoy your ride," he said as he walked back to the small building and flipped a switch.

The balloon began to slowly lift from the ground as the hot gases filled its center. I walked over to the edge of the basket and looked out to see treetops disappearing. I felt Maria as she tucked herself closely into me from behind and wrapped her arms around my waist. I covered her hands with mine and was in absolute heaven when she rested her chin on my shoulder. Every now and then, Maria would raise an arm to point out something of particular interest and would whisper into my ear the sight she was describing.

Maria turned my face toward hers and we shared several soft kisses during our ride, our bodies pressed tightly together in a lover's embrace. The view was fabulous indeed and the feeling of absolute contentment consumed me there in Maria's arms.

As the balloon turned west continuing its circuit, we could see the sun slowly begin to sink toward the horizon. The orange and yellow rays emblazoned the fall foliage and the sky lit up with varying hues of reds, yellows, and orange. It was a romantic moment shared with Maria and she turned me in her arms for a deep kiss.

"Thank you for sharing this moment with me." Her eyes burned dark with passion.

"It has been my pleasure," I answered as I felt my body quivering with excitement.

Maria felt it too. "Are you cold, my love?"

"No, Maria. You have me so aroused, I can no longer control my body," I admitted with a soft blush.

"I promise it will be worth the wait when we return back to the hotel tonight." Then she kissed me deeply again.

I felt like a teenager about to swoon during her first passionate kiss, but Maria held me tight in her arms as we pressed together. The balloon began to descend ending our ride and I knew a memory had been created that would burn deep inside me for the remainder of my life.

Carlos was waiting for us when we landed and assisted us back into the car. We rode back to the new Cultural Center and Maria draped my hand through her elbow as we toured the art exhibits. At the final exhibit, a photographer had captured an image of the exact balloon we had just ridden, and Maria purchased the small photograph for me as a gift to celebrate our ride. I tucked the gift under my arm and we returned to the limo.

Maria treated me to a wonderful steak dinner at a restaurant high above the city and we watched as the lights came alive, illuminating the Twin Cities in all their glory. The day had passed all too quickly in my opinion, but I was eager to return to the hotel to entwine once more in Maria's arms.

When we returned to the suite, she sat me on the bed and began undressing me. She raised the sweater over my head and removed my bra and jeans as my body shook with delight at her touch. When she had me completely naked, she leaned down and softly whispered, "Now I have a gift for you."

I watched with anticipation as Maria walked over to the chair to retrieve two of the small bags she had placed there earlier in the day and carried them to the bed. She opened the first bag and removed a pair of vinyl briefs. She placed my feet through the openings and raised them up my legs. They fit me like a second skin and my eyes grew wide when Maria placed her hand on a small square mounting pad. Whenever she put pressure on the pad, it rubbed across my swollen clit and sent jolts of excitement through my body. Maria smiled at the look on my face and then reached for the second bag. From it she withdrew a long, thick strap-on. After carefully removing it from the package, she pressed the base of the toy onto the mounting pad of my new briefs. The weight of the toy alone as it dangled from the mount sent enough pressure to my clit to send me soaring in ecstasy, but I gritted my teeth to hold back the pleasure my body was experiencing.

Maria reached back into the bag to bring out a tube of lubricant and she opened the top and poured a small amount in her hand. Kneeling down between my legs, she took the toy in her hand and covered the shaft with the smooth lubricant. Up and down her hand moved on the toy sending even more pleasant sensations to my clit and I could no longer hold back the intense climax that ripped through my body as Maria's hand slid down the shaft and her fingers stroked the inside of my thigh.

Maria stood and quickly removed her clothing before joining me on the bed. She pressed herself next to me as her fingers traced small circles around my erect nipples and her mouth covered mine in a soft, teasing kiss. My right hand caressed down her side and across her hip as her tongue swirled inside my mouth. I lifted her left leg and draped it over my thigh, placing the shaft of the toy parallel with the lips of her sex, and the movements of our bodies rubbed the ridged edge against her lips. She moaned deeply in my mouth and her hand cupped my breast, squeezing it as her hips began to squirm.

After several minutes of intense kisses and fondling, I rolled Maria onto her back and rose from the bed. I pulled her to the end of the bed and wrapped her legs around my waist as I bent forward to kiss her. The shaft of the toy rested atop her smooth mound and as our bodies moved, the shaft bounced lightly slapping against her swollen clit. I kissed my way down Maria's neck as my hands squeezed her sensitive breasts, she groaned loudly as she started to roll her hips on the bed. The shaft of the toy was teasing her lips unmercifully and I knew Maria would not take much more before she would be moaning to have it buried deep inside her, but I persisted, waiting for Maria to make her request.

My mouth covered her left breast and I sucked all of it into my mouth, kissing it roughly, as my fingers twisted her other nipple, tugging it as Maria's heels locked behind my hips. Her hands were buried in my dark curls, pulling my mouth my firmly onto her breast as she arched her back. I looked into her dark eyes, they were glowing with lust, and I knew she was close to begging.

"Please, Court, take me now," Maria growled as I bit down on her nipple.

Still sucking her breast, I reached down between us and opened her soaked lips as I gently guided the tip of the shaft into her body. My mouth left her breast and I stood between her quivering thighs. My hands caressed down to her mound, and I could see how tightly her lips spread around the tip of the shaft and I leaned forward slightly placing a hand on each hip. My hands held her body in place as I pressed my hips forward, slowly entering Maria. I watched as inch after inch disappeared into her, and when halfway buried, she gasped loudly, causing me to pause in my stroking.

"Please do not stop, Court, that feels so good," she purred.

I could feel her heels digging into the small of my back as I resumed pressing the shaft deep until it was completely within her. Tears were running down her cheeks, but the smile Maria gave me let me know she was enjoying the feeling of fullness I was giving her. I locked eyes with Maria and slowly began to withdraw the shaft in short, slow strokes, pressing back deeply into her with each forward stroke. Maria bit her lower lip as I lengthened my strokes, plunging back into her as the shaft glided smoothly in her moisture.

Our bodies moved in rhythm as we reached full strokes, the tip barely remaining inside her as our hips slammed together in a dance of wild passion. Perspiration rolled down my face and back as my hips continued to pound against Maria. I could feel her start to tremble as I reached beneath her with my left hand and raised her hips. My right hand lowered to her clit and my palm rubbed furiously across the top of it as she began to wail in pleasure. I could feel her juices coating me each time the shaft was deep inside her and I knew that she was close as her inner muscles pulled at the shaft as they convulsed around it.

My knees threatened to buckle beneath me as I continued to thrust into Maria and then it happened. Just as my legs began to falter, Maria cried out, "Oh God, baby I am coming so hard."

My own body released a shuddering orgasm and I barely had the strength to withdraw from Maria before I collapsed to my knees at the end of the bed. My arms and head rested on Maria's quivering thighs as we both gasped for breath, unable to speak for several minutes.

Maria was the first to recover. She sat up to lift me onto the bed with her and wrapped me in her arms. "You are an incredible lover," she said as her fingers stroked down my face.

"You, my dear, are absolutely beautiful." I returned the smile Maria was wearing.

"I have never felt so amazing, even with my husband." Maria frowned when she saw the change of expression on my face. "I am so sorry. I should not have mentioned him during our time, but Court, you are so much more of a lover to me than he could ever dream of being."

I decided I would deal with the guilt of sleeping with a married woman at a later point and leaned down to kiss Maria, my hands cupping her face as our tongues swirled in a sensual dance. Tears came to my eyes as I realized that our time together was nearly finished. Maria sensed my anxiety, and raised her hands to cover mine and held them close to her.

She broke the kiss and whispered, "This night is nearly done, but our time together is just beginning." She smiled warmly and continued. "If you will have me, I will arrange my travel to allow us to meet as often as we can and share the love we have ignited this weekend." Maria eyes searched mine for some hint of an answer.

"I will take whatever you have to offer."

Maria removed the vinyl briefs and pulled the covers over our exhausted bodies. We fell asleep in one another's arms and dreamed the night away.

The next morning, I awoke alone in the bed again, knowing that Maria had left to return home to her husband. I stretched my stiff body across the bed and rolled over to cuddle the pillow Maria's head had slept on. I could still smell her scent. My eyes came to rest on a small box and a note resting on the bedside table. My eyes filled with tears as I read the note.

> *My Darling Court,*
> *Last night was one of the greatest nights of my life and I look forward to spending many more of them with you. I have left my numbers and a private email address for you and I to communicate and I hope we can plan to be together on your return from Salt Lake. I will be here waiting for you Friday night. Until then, I hope you will wear my gift to you as a pledge of my feelings for you. I love you, Court, and will look forward to seeing you soon.*
> *Maria*

I reached for the small box and opened it to find a gold band with a white gold band entwined around it. Sliding it onto my finger, I felt Maria's arms wrap around me and felt her warm embrace.

With a new energy surrounding me, I got out of the bed and showered. After dressing, I packed my luggage and left the room. Carlos waited for me downstairs and drove me to the airport. As he handed my bag to the porter at the airport, Carlos smiled and said, "I hope to be serving you again very soon, Ms. Lewis."

"Thank you, Carlos, I hope you will be seeing me again this weekend." With a smile, I walked into the terminal, eager to be on my way. As I took my seat in First Class, I glanced over at the empty seat next to me and reclined my seat back to dream of the beautiful woman I had found, in the window seat.

The Dance

A group of her friends had asked Taryn out for drinks after work one Friday evening, and even though she was bone tired from a hard week of manual labor, she intended to keep her promise to join them. Her best friend, Lila, had tried for weeks to drag her out of her small apartment where she had become a recluse after Carol had ended their three-year relationship.

Taryn had come home after work one Friday night to find Carol, as well as over half of the furnishings in the apartment, gone. She found a brief note taped to the refrigerator stating that she was moving in with one of her instructors at the college and, just like that, it was over. Taryn was shell shocked at first, but then realized how much better off she would be without Carol. The woman had done her best to suck Taryn dry both emotionally and financially, and nothing Taryn did was ever good enough.

The shower worked miracles on her physically tired body and, by the time she finished, Taryn felt refreshed and almost eager for a night out with friends. A few beers and some pool might help to improve her mood she thought. She

93

pulled on a pair of Levi's and covered a tank top with a black oxford shirt she left halfway unbuttoned. She slipped on a pair of Harley boots, and walked back into the bathroom to finish her preparations. As she brushed her teeth, she looked at the image staring back at her in the mirror. Her short, salt-and-pepper hair and green eyes were accentuated by a good tan. With a grin of self-approval, Taryn was ready to roll.

She locked the door behind her and slid behind the wheel of her truck. She stopped off at an ATM machine for some cash and, checking the time, found it was almost nine and time for her to meet her friends. The parking lot was jammed when she reached the bar and she circled several rows until she located a spot to park. She opened the bar door and was met by a blast of loud rock music since the DJ had the system cranked. One of her friends waved from the bar and pointed to the billiards area. Taryn paid the cover charge and made her way through the crowd toward her friends. As she wove through the mass of women, she bumped into a small blonde, who turned around and offered Taryn a beautiful smile.

"Excuse me," Taryn said.

"It was my fault, Taryn, I wasn't paying attention to where I was walking," the young woman said.

Taryn looked closely at the woman and realized she had run into Chris, an old friend of Carol's. Taryn felt bad that she didn't recognize her at first. Even worse, she remembered that she and Carol hadn't bothered to go to the funeral of Lucy, Chris's lover who had died from cancer a year ago.

"I didn't recognize you at first, Chris. You look so different. How have you been?" Taryn immediately realized it was a stupid question to ask.

"I have been well thanks, and you? Where is Carol?"

"Carol decided to move on to greener pastures." Taryn blushed slightly.

"I am sorry, Taryn, I didn't know," Chris said with a blush of her own.

"That's all right, Chris, I am slowly adjusting to her being gone," Taryn moved slowly past her. "See you around." She continued to her friends who were waiting for her with cold beer in hand.

Taryn took the offered beer and hugs from the group, leaned back against the wall, and took a deep drink of the icy beer. As she lowered the bottle, her eyes found Chris across the bar and she was again amazed at how different she looked. Maybe she had lightened or cut her hair, but something was definitely different and Taryn found her eyes drawn to her. Chris caught her looking and each time smiled at her, but made no move to make further contact. Taryn shot several games of pool with her friends, but could not concentrate on the game.

"Why don't you go talk to her or ask her to dance," Lila suggested as she caught Taryn smiling at Chris.

"What did you say, Lila?" Taryn realized Lila was speaking to her.

"I said, why don't you go over and talk to her or ask her to dance." Lila chuckled.

"You know, I think I will," Taryn smiled to her friend and walked across the bar to the table where Chris was seated.

Chris smiled warmly at Taryn when she stopped beside her. "Would you care to dance?"

"I would love to." Chris accepted the hand Taryn had offered.

As luck would have it, a slow romantic song began to play as Taryn led Chris onto the dance floor. Taryn took Chris in her arms and smiled when the shorter woman laid her head on her shoulder. Taryn could smell the fruity shampoo that Chris used and felt her body trembling slightly as her arms encircled the smaller woman's waist.

Chris placed her hands on Taryn's back and caressed the strong muscles. Taryn held her close. It felt even better than good to be holding her.

As the song ended and another slow song began, Chris raised her head and looked up into Taryn's green eyes. Taryn saw the pleading look in Chris's eyes and she brought her right hand to lift her chin and leaned down to softly kiss her lips. Taryn felt a surge of excitement rush through her as Chris parted her lips to invite her inside for a deeper kiss. Their tongues swirled together as they moved to the rhythm of the music. Chris pulled Taryn closer.

Taryn could feel a definite tremor through Chris and felt the vibration of a moan in her mouth as they kissed. She felt Chris's hands move down her back and disappear into the back pockets of her jeans as her tongue kissed her hungrily. Taryn could also feel hard nipples as they rubbed cross the front of her body, and she found herself suddenly very turned on by the woman in her arms.

As the song slowed, they ended the kiss. Chris asked, "Would you care to go out on the deck?"

"Sure, Chris." Taryn allowed Chris to lead her down a hall and out a back door. She followed Chris to a picnic table and watched as she sat down on the top of the table and then pulled Taryn between her spread legs, locking her legs around her thighs.

Chris placed her hands on Taryn's hips and pulled her tightly into her body as she leaned in to kiss her again. She boldly took Taryn's hand and placed it on her breast.

Taryn could feel the swollen nipple as it pressed against the soft fabric of her blouse, her fingers slowly circled it, and Chris began to moan.

Their kisses grew more heated as their hands began to explore each other. Chris raised the hem of her blouse and guided Taryn's hand underneath to caress the soft mounds of her breasts as she ground her hips against Taryn. They could hear the music from inside the bar as the pulsing rhythm matched the rocking of Taryn's hips as her hands teased Chris's excited nipples.

"I need more of you, Taryn," Chris managed to breathe between urgent kisses. "Will you take me home?"

Taryn took Chris by the hand and led her out a side gate and to her truck. She closed the door behind her and climbed behind the wheel, thankful that her apartment was not far away. Chris scooted close to her, kissed her neck, and rubbed the length of her thigh as she drove, making it difficult for Taryn to focus on the road ahead.

When they arrived at the apartment, Taryn unlocked the door and followed Chris inside. She tossed her keys onto a small table before leading Chris to the bedroom. She sat Chris on the edge of the bed and knelt down to unbutton her blouse and slide it over her shoulders as Chris's hands unfastened her jeans. She raised her hips off the bed to allow Taryn to pull them down her legs and Taryn smiled to find her bare underneath as she tossed the jeans across the room.

Chris's hands pulled the hem of Taryn's shirt out of her jeans and slid the shirt and wife beater over her head in one fluid motion. Chris pulled her to her feet and her hands unfastened and slid the jeans down as Taryn stepped out of her boots.

Taryn pressed her back onto the bed and lay down next to her, propping herself on an elbow. Her right hand began at Chris's neck and slowly caressed its way down her body as she watched Chris's eyes for a reaction to her touches. Each time her hand neared one of Chris's breasts she arched her back, filling Taryn's hands with excited flesh. When her hand moved lower, Chris's hips squirmed under her touch, begging Taryn to continue her stroking.

Taryn moved further up the bed and leaned down to kiss Chris as her fingers continued to knead and gently tug at her aching breasts. She pressed a thigh between Chris's and could feel her dampness as Chris ground into her. Taryn kissed her way across her neck and began to nibble lightly on her ear lobe.

Taryn's warm breath in her ear and her hand on her breast was making Chris delirious with need. She dragged her nails up Taryn's back and sighed deeply when Taryn moved to lower her body onto hers. Taryn could feel her mound as it settled onto Chris and their bodies began a sensual dance to a rhythm known only to their bodies as they entwined and moved together in harmony. Chris locked her heels around Taryn's thighs and used her leverage to thrust into Taryn, and her breathing became gasps for air. She could feel the tremors turn to shudders as she reached climax and she cried out in pleasure.

Taryn kissed down to her breasts, her mouth engulfing one as her hand moved down between them. She parted Chris's lips to rub across the top of her clit.

"Touch me," Chris said as Taryn's teeth grazed her nipple.

Taryn pressed her fingers between soaked lips and entered Chris slowly, burying three fingers deep inside her needy body.

"Oh God, yes," Chris cried out as Taryn curled her fingers deep inside and her thumb rubbed across her clit. Chris buried her hands in Taryn's hair holding her mouth firmly in place as Taryn began to slide her fingers in and out. She could feel her juices trickling down the inside of Chris's thighs. As Taryn stroked faster and deeper, Chris's hips matched the tempo.

Taryn could feel the muscles as they contracted around her fingers and knew that Chris was again close to climaxing. She turned her fingers sideways, stretching Chris wide with each stroke. She felt Chris convulse with contractions, releasing a flood of juices as she came again.

Taryn was throbbing for release and she turned to position her mound above Chris. She lowered her mouth to taste Chris's wetness, and drank deeply, her tongue probing deeply as her fingers rubbed across her twitching clit. Taryn lowered herself onto Chris's mouth and groaned loudly as she felt her tongue slide deeply inside. Chris's tongue drove in and out of Taryn as she eagerly lapped the juices flowing freely and soon both women were lost in a frenzy of lust as tongues, fingers, and hips danced a wild rhythm until they climaxed together and collapsed in a pile on the bed.

Taryn moved beside Chris and turned her onto her side, snuggling around her, an arm encircling her protectively. Chris turned her head toward Taryn and they shared a tender kiss to celebrate the passion they had shared. She took Taryn's hand in hers, and pressed it between her breasts and, entwined, they fell into an exhausted sleep.

Hips, Lips, and Fingertips

Chris arrived home and eagerly rushed to her computer to check her email, knowing that Kate would be home later tonight and there would be instructions for her arrival waiting. They had been lovers for several months, primarily on weekends. They both traveled in their careers, which severely limited the time they could spend together, mostly to weekends. The absence during the week only increased their sexual appetite for each other and Chris eagerly awaited her lover's return.

She poured herself a glass of white wine as the computer booted up, and when she sat down at her desk, she smiled as a message flashed notifying her that she had new mail. She opened up the mail to read the following note.

My Darling Chris,

My flight lands at four and I should be home around five at the latest. When I arrive, I want to see you dressed in your thick robe and nothing else. So when you arrive home pour yourself a nice glass of wine and kick back until I arrive. I can't wait to devour you. ☺

Love,

Kate

Chris felt a rush of wetness between her thighs as she read her note. Kate was a very creative lover and Chris always looked forward to each new adventure with her. She glanced at the clock. Thirty more minutes and Kate would be home. She sipped her wine and allowed her imagination to wander in anticipation of her lover's arrival.

Kate tossed her bag in the trunk of her car and, with a wicked gleam in her eyes, drove for home. She could taste Chris's juices on the tip of her tongue as her foot pressed harder on the gas pedal. Just a few more minutes now and she would be there. Her dampness grew with each passing mile. Her body ached to be kissed and fondled by her lover. She had such great plans for taking her slowly and completely, but she knew she would have to please her first and quickly to relieve her aching body and allow her to concentrate on seducing Chris's mind and body. As she turned into the drive, she could hear the racing of her heart as it beat wildly in her chest and felt the throb deep between her thighs.

Chris heard the click of the key in the lock and then the twist of the knob as Kate arrived home. She found her seated on the couch and walked up in front of her.

"Hello, my darling," Kate said, with a husky voice filled with need.

"Welcome home, sweetie."

She followed Kate's movements as she dropped her bag and sat beside her on the couch, then took her in her arms for a slow deep kiss. Chris melted into her as her hands teased her body and her tongue swirled inside her mouth. Kate broke the kiss, and took her by the hand leading her through the bedroom into the bathroom. She sat her on the edge of the tub and smiled up at her with a naughty grin.

Chris watched Kate step back, kick off her loafers and begin unbuttoning the sleeves of the royal blue oxford she was wearing. Standing in front of her, Kate loosened each button while Chris's hands made quick work of the braided belt and fastener of Kate's tan chinos before her fingers slid the zipper down to reveal tan bare skin as she slowly slipped the pants down Kate's hips and off her body.

When Kate had finished unbuttoning her shirt, Chris watched it slide down her shoulders, and fall to the floor along with her pants. She reached behind her and pulled the snug fitting sports bra over her head, leaving her beautifully naked in front of her lover. Her insides were bristling with sensation as Chris's eyes slowly devoured her. She could wait no longer. She needed to come fast and hard.

She buried her fingers in Chris's hair and pulled her face onto her swollen breast. "Oh yes, don't be afraid to suck them hard, lover," she panted as Chris's mouth licked her nipple before sucking all of her deep into her hot waiting mouth. Her hands roamed over Kate's body as her tongue teased and her teeth nibbled at the swollen nipple. Their moans combined to echo in the bathroom. Her hand moved Chris's mouth to her other breast as her hands cupped the sensitive flesh, caressing it with loving strokes.

Kate could feel the wetness as it flowed down the inner part of her thigh as her excitement continued to grow. Her clit throbbed as she forced Chris's head down her body and raised one foot to rest on the edge of the tub to give her lover access to her most delicious spot. Chris parted her lips with the tip of her tongue as her lover's hips began to rock into her face. She had never seen Kate turned on like this before and her obvious need for relief tempted Chris to tease her. Her growls quickly put an end to the teasing as Kate placed her lover's mouth firmly on her clit. The taste of her excitement sparked the lust inside Chris and she sucked her clit deep into her mouth as she penetrated her lips with three fingers, gliding smoothly into her lover.

Kate threw her head back in wild pleasure as Chris licked her into a frenzy and her fingers drove deeply inside her. Violent spasms raced as a powerful orgasm ripped through her, leaving her speechless and panting. Chris lightly kissed her clit and then stood before her, taking her face in her hands, kissing her deeply, sharing the taste of her juices with her lover.

Temporarily sated, Kate sat Chris back on the edge of the tub and opened the sash of her robe. Kate stepped over to the vanity, picked up a small cordless clipper, and knelt in front of her. She spread her thighs wide as her thumb flipped the switch and the clippers buzzed to life. With careful, loving hands, she trimmed the damp hairs from Chris's entire pubic area, catching the hairs in her left hand as they fell from her quivering body.

Satisfied that she was properly trimmed, Kate disposed of the hairs and placed the clippers back on the vanity. She picked up a small bottle of baby oil and poured a small amount in her hand. She coated Chris's mound with the silky oil and then stood to draw bathwater for her lover. Chris stood and Kate removed the loose robe from around her and hung it next to the shower. She took a mouthful of the wine and shared it with Chris as they kissed deeply waiting for the tub to fill.

Kate guided her into the tub filled halfway with warm water and then entered to sit at the front of the tub facing her. There was a wicked glint in her eyes as she reached down and picked up Chris's right foot in her hand and lifted it to rest on her left shoulder. She picked up a can of shaving cream, placing a large dollop in her hands and began spreading it down Chris's thigh to her ankle. She picked up a fresh razor, and beginning at the top of her thigh began shaving her leg in long, smooth strokes, leaving her leg smooth as satin. She lowered her leg back into the water, rinsing it carefully before performing the same action with her left leg.

Finally, clean-shaven from the hips down, she lifted Chris to once again sit on the edge of the tub as she sat cross-legged in front of her. Chris watched in anticipation as she reached for a bar of soft soap and lathered her hands. Kate leaned forward and covered the remaining hair on her mound with the silky soap. She picked up a fresh razor and, starting above her mound, slowly shaved the closely trimmed hairs until Chris's skin was bare and smooth. Her strokes continued down the sides of her swollen lips and, once satisfied with the smoothness, Kate placed the fingers of her left hand inside Chris's lips to carefully trim the last of the hairs. Then she rubbed her hand over the slick, smooth mound and smiled up to her.

Draining the tub, Kate turned on the water to rinse their bodies in the shower. She patted Chris dry with a soft thick towel and again placed her on the side of the tub. She stepped over to the vanity, picked up a long, royal-blue silk scarf, and covered Chris's eyes, tying it snuggly behind her head.

"Are you ready for some loving?" Kate whispered into her ear.

"Oh yes, please." Chris barely breathed as Kate stood her up and led her into the bedroom.

Kate laid her on her back, spread eagle on the bed, and using additional silk scarves, began to restrain her arms and legs to the frame of the bed. She smiled as she watched

Chris' nipples swell to life as the silk brushed her body lightly.

"Does that feel good, baby?"

"Wonderful," she said as Kate tied the last scarf to the bedframe.

She crawled up beside Chris and sat beside her. She leaned forward and reached under a pillow to pull out a feather duster with long, blue feathers attached to a short handle. Starting at her neck, she swirled the feathers lightly over her hypersensitive skin, down across her nipples and down her sides. Chris's moans echoed in the room with each new stroke of the feathers. Chill bumps covered her body even though the room was quite warm as Kate continued to tease her lover.

She moved the feather duster down to her right foot and swirled the feathers up the inside of her leg to the top of her thigh. As she turned to stroke down her leg, the tips of the feathers brushed across her bare mound and Chris gasped at the sensation. Kate turned the duster so the sleek, wooden handle eased across her clit and she moaned with delight at the firmness of its touch against her. Kate watched as juice began to slip past her lips to slide down the insides of her thighs.

"You are so wet, my love," she purred as the handle slid down Chris's slick outer lips.

"You are driving me insane," Chris groaned. "I need you to make me come soon."

"That will not be a problem," Kate promised as the feathers brushed down her left leg and back up the inside of her thigh.

Kate reached under the pillow yet again and pulled out a long dildo with thick ridges down its sides. "You should really enjoy this." She laid the dildo across her swollen lips dragging it slowly down while turning it to coat it with her juices.

Chris' hips squirmed as the ridges of the dildo rubbed across her lips and clit. "Can't wait to have that inside me," she breathed as Kate took the feather duster and pressed the handle into the hole in the base of the dildo.

She spread Chris' lips with soft fingertips as she placed the head of the dildo just inside her opening. She penetrated her with an inch of the shaft, stretching her lips wide with the sex toy before sliding back out. The placement of the feather duster, made the feathers kiss the inside of her thigh, making her squeal with delight. With each following stroke, the dildo slipped deeper inside her body until Kate was making full loving strokes with the toy and the feathers swirled the full length of her thigh.

Chris's hips arched up from the bed in harmony with each stroke and she began to quiver with delight as Kate moved faster and deeper inside her, thrusting full strokes as she fucked her wildly. Kate leaned forward, and slowly licked the underside of her breasts and then began to flick the tip of her tongue across blood-gorged nipples. Chris's breaths were becoming more ragged as the wave began to swell inside her and Kate knew that it would not take much longer at this pace to send her tremoring in orgasm. She continued to thrust deeply into her lover as she bent her head down and circled Chris's clit with her tongue as she thrashed wildly on the bed.

"Oh yes, kiss it," she begged as Kate continued to tease her lover. The arching of her hips had increased as her body urged her lover to make her come. Sensing she was very close, Kate covered Chris's clit with her mouth and sucked her deeply into her mouth, trapping her clit against the roof of her mouth with a relentless tongue as her climax overtook her.

"I'm coming," was all Chris could say. They were the only words needed as Kate pounded into her with fast strokes and nibbled the top of her clit with sharp teeth. Chris' hips thrashed in pleasure for several minutes before her orgasm started to wane. Kate slowed her strokes to a halt and then reached down to untie Chris's ankles. She slowly withdrew the dildo from her throbbing body and then untied her wrists and removed the blindfold from her eyes.

"Are you ready for another?" she asked with a wicked grin. The smile on Chris' face gave her the answer she was hoping to receive.

"Roll over and up on your knees," Kate instructed.

Kate spread her knees wide on the bed and bent down to run her flat tongue down the length of her lips from behind. "Mmm still very wet," Kate said as she pulled the feather duster from the dildo and slid two fingers deep into its base.

She slid underneath Chris's body and took one of her dangling breasts into her mouth as her fingers parted her soaked lips and she slid the dildo in deep. Chris groaned as she rocked her hips back into the dildo as it slid deeply inside her. Kate toyed with her nipple as she allowed her to set the pace and rhythm while she held the toy firmly in place. Her body still primed from her last orgasm, Chris rocked faster and faster until she was thrusting fully onto the ribbed toy, each new stroke building on the wave coursing through her.

Kate's fingers brushed across Chris's clit in small circles as she began to cry out in pleasure. "Yes, yes, yes," she groaned as she slammed into the dildo and came intensely on top of Kate before collapsing into her waiting arms.

Kate slid the dildo from her and held her close as the tremors ran through her lover. Tears flowed down Chris's cheek as her breathing began to return to normal and she found comfort in her lover's arms. Laying her head on Kate's shoulder, she could hear the beating of Kate's heart as it pounded against her chest. Wordlessly she closed her eyes and allowed the rhythm of Kate's breathing to draw her into a deep, totally satisfied sleep. A smile played on their lips as the two lovers lay entwined in each other's arms dreaming of nights yet to come.

Landfall

Tricia Evans climbed to the top of the lighthouse and frowned when she saw the massive clouds that were roiling angrily in the Pensacola sky. For days now, she had anxiously awaited the approach of Hurricane Ivan as he threatened the entire Gulf Coast. She had completed all her preparations so all she could do now was remain calm and pray that she and her beloved lighthouse survived the storm.

For several years, Tricia had been the full time keeper for the lone lighthouse that serviced the area. A bit on the eccentric side, she maintained the aging lighthouse and took advantage of the excellent lighting and scenery to paint in oils and watercolors to supplement her keeper's salary. A local gallery exhibited her work and her paintings sold as quickly as she could produce them.

Tricia maintained a solitary existence; her only steady companion was Kiki, a black cat that she had rescued from a dumpster when she was a scrawny little kitten. Kiki would follow her everywhere, in the lighthouse or outside around the grounds, and would doze in the windowsill as Tricia painted at the top of the building. Today Kiki remained closer to her than ever. It was as if she could feel Tricia's anxiety regarding the storm, and remained closer than ever to her two-legged companion. As Tricia gazed out at the rough water, Kiki jumped up to the windowsill and stretched her paws up to Tricia's shoulders, purring loudly. Chuckling, Tricia took the fully grown cat into her arms and snuggled the purring beast.

"It's going to be a rough one," Tricia told her companion who was gazing up at her with bright yellow eyes. "Don't worry though, my friend, we have enough Cat Chow to last for a month."

Kiki seemed comforted by the words spoken to her and began licking the fingers that were scratching under her neck, a loving gesture from feline to human. Tricia checked the light mechanism, and content that all was in order, she and Kiki made their way back down the steps to the keeper's cottage.

†

It was nearly five before Carmen Sanchez made her way from her dental practice back to her home on Grand Pointe. The traffic was a nightmare as panicked residents began to flee the coastal town. The latest on the weather predicted Ivan would move ashore east of Pensacola therefore sparing the new house Carmen had built just west of there. Her home was built to all the state codes, and she was confident it would be safe, especially since the storm was bearing down farther east. With a fully stocked pantry and plenty of gas for the generator, the young Canadian dentist settled in for the storm. She made a quick dinner and a pot of coffee before heading upstairs to the master loft to ride out her first storm.

Settling into a comfortable chaise lounge, Carmen sipped at her coffee as she watched the angry sea pound the coastline. Predicted to make a landfall around two in the morning, Ivan would leave residents in total darkness as the storm unleashed its fury. Carmen wondered for the first time if she had made a mistake in leaving the relative safety of frigid Canada for the unpredictable Florida weather.

Watching the trees sway violently in the increasing wind made Carmen shiver and she rose to get a blanket to cover herself in the chaise. She turned on the television and surfed to the local channel for weather information. Carmen stopped in her tracks as the newscaster reported that Ivan had taken a more westerly shift and had increased to a Category Five storm. She realized that this would be devastating to any area subject to a landfall. Her blood ran cold in her veins as she realized the time to evacuate safely had passed several hours ago. Now her fate rested with the mercy of the storm.

Her dinner threatened to revisit as she listened to the continued report, and Carmen turned the volume down to decrease her anxiety as she wrapped herself in a warm blanket and snuggled back into the chaise. With nothing more she could do to ensure her safety, she decided to try to keep her mind occupied as the storm approached. She picked up the book she had been reading for several nights, but she was unable to concentrate enough to read. Frustrated, she returned the book to the table and laid her head back on the chaise in an effort to relax.

†

Tricia hovered over the old couch watching the weather reports on television, unable to sit through the broadcast as the forecast showed Ivan now approaching the Gulf Shores area. She climbed the seventy-three steps of the lighthouse to look out across water that, until this morning, had been a flat, glassy surface. Now the growing, twenty-foot waves chewed violently at the jetties and piers along the coast. She watched as the skies above the Naval Air Station lit up in a brilliant fluorescent green as the winds and heavy rain bands began to come on shore, ripping trees from the ground as transformers exploded and homes became lost to the darkness. The eerie glow in the sky remained and Tricia took several shots with her digital camera, and she bent down to check that the video camera was capturing the violent action of the storm.

The winds howled loudly as they directed their force at the lighthouse, their pitch rising to an earsplitting level with each gust. Kiki trembled in Tricia's arms as they watched water spouts form in the Gulf and begin to move onshore, thrashing about the helpless homes on the coastline, ripping them from their foundations in mere seconds. Sickened by the massive destruction she was witnessing, she carried Kiki back down the steps and away from the large, exposed glass panels. Tricia imagined she could feel the foot-thick concrete walls shiver as she descended the tower. Certain they were built strongly enough to weather the storm, she chuckled at her wild imagination.

The television broadcaster announced that power outages were rapidly increasing as Ivan approached, and that massive flooding was occurring in the downtown area. Forty-foot waves had destroyed large sections on the Interstate 10 Bridge and the Three Mile Bridge leading to Gulf Breeze, stranding anyone trying to make a last-minute escape from the low-lying island community.

God bless anyone out in this storm, Tricia thought as the lights flickered and the power failed. "One, two, three, four, five," she slowly counted out loud, as she waited for the standby generator to start. At six, she held her breath as she heard the rumbling of the engine, and exhaled as the generator roared to life bringing power back to the keeper's cottage and the lamps of the lighthouse. God forbid there would be anyone foolish enough to be on the water in this weather, but if there were, she and the lighthouse would serve as their guiding light.

The television twitched and then came back to life and Tricia flipped to find a local station. Only one out of five had a signal strong enough to reach the viewing public as Ivan's winds wreaked havoc on any structure standing in their way, gutting buildings and toppling trees without prejudice.

She looked down at her watch. "One thirty and the worst has yet to come." She could hear the raindrops pelting the panels upstairs, a sound closer to rocks striking a tin roof than water hitting glass. Tricia felt confident that the panels would survive the wind, as long as no flying debris impacted directly on them. She paced the floor, stopping to stare at a now snowy screen, the voice in the set fading and then disappearing totally from earshot. She pushed the button on the remote to kill the power as a large crash sounded outside. Peering through the small glass window on the front door she could determine that one of the large, century oaks had split in the high winds and a large section had crashed to the ground.

Tricia had lived in Florida all of her life, but she never grew accustomed to the fury Mother Nature could force upon land, sea, human, and animal at any given moment. The winds rumbled deep, like a freight train, and she knew that tornados were spawning, adding to the destruction of the storm surge, with sustained winds of one hundred thirty miles per hour. Silently praying for daylight and the storm to end, Tricia continued to pace.

†

Carmen had fallen to sleep in the chaise and the loud explosion of electrical transformers startled her awake. She woke to total darkness, disorientation plaguing her until her eyes adjusted to the lack of light. She reached down to press a button on her watch to illuminate the face and saw that it was one thirty in the morning. The winds were howling outside as they pounded against her home and she felt a huge draft coming up the stairs. Cautiously she stood and started toward the staircase to descend and search for damage. She was certain by the amount of draft that she had lost at least one of the large windows downstairs that faced the Gulf. As she stepped down on the first step, Tricia could hear the Venetian blinds flailing against the wall, and the sound of furniture forcibly dragged across the wooden floors.

Carmen froze in her tracks when she reached the midway point of her stairway and a lightning flash illuminated her living room. Nothing she had ever experienced could have prepared her for this moment. The entire front section of her first floor was gutted by the storm surge and the force of the winds had combined to scatter furniture and belongings throughout the house. Floodwaters were rising quickly in the living room and Carmen turned to run back up the stairs just as the remaining fragments of the front windows exploded.

When she reached the master loft again, she walked cautiously toward the main window and squinted into the darkness. She looked in both directions to find the only parts left of her neighbors' homes were the foundations wiped clean by the forceful surge. Debris littered the streets and yards of what had previously been a pristine neighborhood, and Carmen's shock began to set in.

The explosion of a transformer startled Carmen and her mind raced, searching for the correct course of action. Fleeing her home was certainly a desperate decision, but remaining would be almost certain death as the waves continued to pulverize the quickly deteriorating walls of her home. As if on cue, a large wave crushed the front of her house with a blow that broke off the corner of her house and flung her backward against the wall. Battered and bruised, Carmen rose and began to fight her way back toward the staircase, battling the wind that threatened to sweep her off her feet. Her heart pounded in her chest as she fumbled her way through the darkness to descend the stairs, the cold water surrounding her trembling body. Every step took tremendous effort as Carmen strained against the pull of the current that was trying to draw her out of the house and into the dangerous flow.

Reaching the first floor, Carmen headed for the rear of the house hoping to put as much distance between her and the coastline as possible. Praying that she would safely reach higher land, Carmen forced the back door open. She was immediately pelted in the face by spray as the water reversed its path, and headed back to sea. Carmen timed her movements to the ebb and flow of the waters, and when she felt, the water was at its lowest point she began wading through the knee-deep water.

What remained of the houses in the area looked like ghastly skeletons in the deep darkness of the storm as Carmen fought against the strong current. There was no other human in sight, and the raging waters adding to the weight of her weary heart, Carmen feared that the storm had killed all of her neighbors. Her heart sank further when an object brushed into her hip and she reached down to pick up a soaked teddy bear owned by the blonde-haired, two-year-old girl who lived next door. Carmen called out, her voice muted by the screeching of the wind, the force of it nearly capturing Carmen's breath as she struggled to move.

Must keep moving Carmen screamed in her mind in an attempt to clear the fog that was rapidly moving into her consciousness. All her effort had barely moved her a half block away from the Gulf and she was quickly losing the battle to the rising water. As she fought to take her next step, a broken limb from a nearby tree struck her from behind. The searing pain in her ribs expelled the breath she had in her lungs and she gasped to take in new air. Her head began to swim and Carmen passed out falling forward onto a plank of roofing torn from an unknown building. Unconscious and bleeding, her body began to drift.

Carmen awoke an hour later to a throbbing headache. Every time she tried to lift her head, a blinding pain would nearly cause her to lose consciousness again, and Carmen feared that worse than the pain. She lay prone on the section of roofing and felt the drifting of the board in the water. Attempts to roll over to her side brought stabbing pains from her badly bruised and possibly cracked ribs. Her eyes searched the surrounding darkness for anything that looked familiar, but there were no landmarks left to aid Carmen in her orientation. Exhausted, bruised, and battered, Carmen laid her cheek back onto the rough grit of the shingles and allowed her eyes to close.

Carmen didn't know how long she'd been asleep this time and managed to raise her head long enough to catch a glimpse of the beam of light coming from the lighthouse. Her heart raced with the knowledge of where she was, and she was further comforted to find the section of roofing was being pulled in the direction of the lighthouse by the current. The rain continued to whip down on the tender skin of her bruised cheeks so she once again laid her head down.

†

Tricia could pace no more so she carefully climbed the steps back up to the lighthouse. The panels had held up to the worst of the winds, but the rain was pounding so hard that visibility was minimal. She could briefly see the white caps of waves as they battered half way up the lighthouse walls. It was three o'clock, a mere hour after Ivan's eye had made landfall, and yet it seemed an eternity to her. The heavy rains and wave action continued. However, the winds appeared to be slowly losing strength. *Only a few more hours until sunrise.* Her eyes scanned the darkness.

Exhausted from the stress, Tricia lay down on her bed and instinctively reached out for Kiki who was lying closely beside her. Burying her fingers in the soft fur of her companion, she collapsed into exhausted sleep.

After an hour of restful sleep, Tricia began tossing and turning so she decided she might as well be up and moving about. She went into her tiny kitchen to make a pot of coffee and to set out food for Kiki. Filling the largest mug available, she once again headed up the stairs to the lighthouse. The beam was still running strong, sending its signal deep into the night. Settling into a comfortable chair, she sipped her coffee and waited for the sun to rise. The rain still pelted the large glass panels as she peered across the water.

Tricia caught herself dozing as the rhythmic pelting of the rain had the same effect as rain on a tin roof during a summer storm. Kiki had finished her meal and was walking along the windowsills, performing her own version of feline pacing.

She was watching Kiki when she suddenly crouched down and began staring out one of the windows. Kiki's tail began twitching in the same manner it did when she was stalking a squirrel or bird from the safety of her home. She chuckled at Kiki's behavior and stood to see what Kiki was stalking.

The first vision that Tricia saw was the brilliance of the horizon. Bright red, yellow, and orange streaks were starting to glow as the sun prepared for its arrival in the east. Storm clouds heavy with rain were still plentiful, but the presence of the brilliant colors gave her hope that the storm would pass today. As she walked to where Kiki sat staring they were both startled when a sheet of rain hit the glass panel, but Kiki was

117

intent on her prey and refused to leave her spot at the window. Tricia tried to focus her eyes beyond the raindrops straining to see what had grabbed Kiki's attention so intently. Patiently she allowed her eyes to focus on the area of Kiki's interest and slowly an object began to appear. Tricia wiped her eyes in disbelief that she had just seen a piece of roofing with someone on top of it, floating in the agitated surf, but sure enough that was what she was looking at.

Kiki looked up at her as if to ask, *do you see it, Mom?* Tricia answered, "I see it, Kiki."

Setting her mug down on the table, she headed down the stairs toward the front door. The area where the object was floating would normally have been about a waist deep, but Tricia was cautious, knowing that it could be much deeper from the storm. She stopped to grab a tethered rescue ring just in case. Bracing against the wind, she opened the front door and stepped out into an environment she hardly recognized. The densely wooded area surrounding the lighthouse looked like a war zone. The large century oaks were split or totally uprooted, and the smaller trees flattened to the ground. Debris from the surrounding communities mounded up in large piles and the water was full of floating debris. Several boats had broken free of their moorings and were scattered amongst the piles like a child's toys.

Turning toward the surf, her face was pelted by heavy rain. She could barely see the object still floating in the surf, now about a hundred yards away from the lighthouse. There was no observable movement on the floating debris as she dropped down into the storm-chilled water.

Tricia tried calling out to the person on the make-shift raft, but her voice was lost in the howling of the wind. As she feared, the action of the waves had caused erosion along the shoreline and she swiftly sank to her chest in the churning water. Holding tight to the rescue ring, Tricia began swimming toward the floating object, praying the current didn't shift and take it farther out to sea. The dangerous current began taking its toll on her as she battled waves and exhaustion. She lifted her arm to take a stroke and a piece of jagged debris struck her right cheek opening a gash in the tender skin. Tricia felt the warmth of her blood as it mixed with the rain and flowed down her face. The stinging from the salt as it reached the wound helped her stay focused as she swam ever closer to the floating object.

As she approached, she could see the dark curls matted against the head of the person as the raft bounced and recoiled in the stormy waters. There still was no sign of movement as Tricia called out with all her force, "Hello, hello."

Tricia was excited to see movement and increased her speed as she swam with renewed vigor. Within minutes, she had reached the floating debris and a young woman looked up, her eyes pleading for help.

"Just hang on," Tricia said as she saw the pain and exhaustion in the young woman's face.

Carmen thought she heard someone calling out 'hello' in this horrible weather. *I must be hallucinating.* She struggled to raise her throbbing head and with swollen eyes, she saw a figure swimming toward her. She moved her mouth to speak, but her body was so weak she was unable to form any words.

When the stranger was carefully trying to transfer her to the rescue ring, Carmen, for a brief moment, resisted. Letting go of the one object that had kept her alive for an unknown amount of time while being tossed through the rough waves was terrifying. Finally placing her trust in this stranger, Carmen let go of the floating debris and clung to the ring.

Tricia called upon the last of her own energy supplies to swim through white-capping waves to take the woman to shore. Struggling against the violent waves and breathing in ragged gasps, Tricia felt a great sense of relief when she could finally touch bottom again and move onto shore. She carefully lifted the woman in her arms and walked as smoothly as she could back to the lighthouse. Kiki was waiting at the door, and followed them as she led the woman into the bathroom.

The woman grimaced with every movement, but Tricia was able to remove the soaked clothing while she drew the last of the hot water for a bath. The woman trembled as she helped her into the tub and began to assess the numerous injuries. There were angry bruises along the woman's rib cage and deep breaths were obviously painful for her. Tricia gently touched the area tracing the length of each bone and was relieved to find that the bones felt intact. The woman suffered from numerous scrapes and scratches, but the bruised ribs seemed to be the most dangerous of her injuries. The woman continued to shiver as Tricia carefully bathed her body, pouring the warm water over her in an attempt to warm her. The woman tried to speak several times but the shivering and exhaustion kept her mute.

"My name is Tricia and you are safe now," she promised trying to ease the woman's tortured psyche as she tended to her wounds.

Tricia had forgotten about her own injury in her rush to save the woman until a shaking hand arose from the water to softly stroke her cheek. The damaged flesh was sensitive, but the tenderness of the woman's touch made all the pain disappear and the smile she managed brought tears to Tricia's eyes. After the trauma the woman had experienced this night, she still managed a smile that made her eyes shine brightly.

Flushing from the woman's touch, Tricia laid her back in the tub to soak as she disappeared from the room returning moments later with sweats, thick socks, and her warmest robe. She helped the woman to a standing position and rested her arm around her as she stepped out of the tub. She gently patted the woman dry and helped her into the clothes.

"Would you like some coffee?"

The woman nodded and was able to squeak out a weak *yes* as Tricia led her into the bedroom and sat her down on the bed, propping pillows behind her back.

"I will be right back." As she turned to walk to the kitchen, Kiki trotted past her and jumped onto the bed and walked directly up to the woman and crawled into her lap. Chuckling, Tricia said, "That shy creature is Kiki, queen of this castle."

She poured two large mugs of coffee and carried them into the bedroom. The woman gratefully accepted the steaming mug and slowly sipped the tasty offering.

"Thanks, my name is Carmen, and I appreciate all you have done for me." Tears filled her eyes.

"Nice to meet you, Carmen. I am glad Kiki saw you and we were able to help." She stretched and scratched the purring cat.

"Thank you too, Kiki." Carmen reached down to pat the cat, her fingers brushing Tricia's making her flush even deeper.

Carmen closely inspected the cut. "You have a nasty cut on your cheek that needs some attention. If you will clean it and bring me some small bandages, I will butterfly it for you. You could probably use a few stitches, but I don't think you will be getting them anytime soon."

Tricia walked to the bathroom to tend to the cut and rummaged through the medicine cabinet to find small bandages as instructed. She handed them to Carmen as she gently sat on the edge of the bed next to her. Her heart raced as Carmen softly sealed the wound with gentle expertise.

Carmen took her totally by surprise when she took her face in her soft hands and brushed her cheek with a tender kiss.

Carmen sat back against the pillows as she sipped the coffee and Tricia could see the weariness overcome her. She took the coffee from her hands and helped her slide down the bed before tucking the covers around her stiff and sore body. She then turned out the light and took fresh clothes into the bathroom for a quick shower to wash the salt and debris from her own exhausted body.

As she stepped out of the bathroom, she heard her name called softly. "Tricia, will you come hold me?"

Without speaking, Tricia slipped between the warm covers and carefully wrapped her arm around Carmen's shoulder as she snuggled deep into the woman's soft body.

Tricia could hear the pounding of her heart as Carmen's body relaxed partially on top of her, and she feared rest would escape her tortured body, but the warmth of Carmen slowly drained the last of her energy and she drifted into sweet sleep.

The storm raged on outside while two exhausted women and one curiously content cat slept the morning away.

†

Carmen woke first and closely watched the sleeping woman who had saved her life. Shallow laugh lines framed the sparkling blue eyes that had caressed her as Tricia gently bathed her battered body mere hours ago. A smile played on her face as she dreamed and dimples made her smile irresistible to Carmen. Her fingertips played softly along the lines of Tricia's well-tanned face. Satisfied that the woman was real, Carmen laid her head back on her shoulder and slept for several more hours.

She heard the audible sound of Tricia's stomach growling and slipped her hand under her shirt. When her fingertips stroked across the flat stomach she heard a sharp gasp.

"Someone sounds hungry." Carmen continued to stroke across her stomach and she lifted her head to look into Tricia's eyes. "I can make a mean omelet, if you have power and the right ingredients," Carmen offered.

"How about gas and a fully stocked refrigerator, will that work?"

"Will you let me cook for you, then?"

"That would be great." Tricia closed her eyes as if she were savoring the last few touches.

Carmen slowly and painfully raised her body from the bed, grimacing with each new movement.

"Are you sure you wouldn't rather relax and let me cook breakfast?" Tricia asked with a note of concern in her voice.

"After all you have done for me, breakfast is the least I can do."

"I need to make a quick trip upstairs to make sure everything survived the storm, but I will try to hurry." Tricia stood and walked Carmen to the door of the kitchen. "Make yourself at home and I will be right back."

Tricia looked down at her wrist to find that it was two in the afternoon and her feet barely touched the steps as she bounded up to the tower. Her light mood was considerably darkened, however, when she reached the top of the steps and looked out at the ruined landscape surrounding her in all directions. Dark clouds traveled low in the sky as a light rain fell and the wind continued to blow. Ivan was traveling inland now, but had left a wake of devastation behind that would take years to overcome. Searching the horizon for familiar landmarks and finding few, she returned to the task of surveying damages to her precious lighthouse. Fortunately, the structure remained strong and the light's beam cut through the clouds, diligently performing its tireless duty.

As she slowly descended the stairs and entered the kitchen, she could hear Carmen humming to herself as she beat eggs for omelets. Dark curls piled atop the robe, and bounced across her shoulders, as Carmen worked on breakfast.

"Anything I can do, besides stay out of your way?"

"How about making a fresh pot of coffee?"

Tricia started the pot of coffee and then leaned back on the counter to watch Carmen as she moved gracefully through the kitchen.

Carmen gingerly removed the heavy robe. "I was beginning to wonder if I would ever get warm again." Carmen handed the robe to her.

Tricia took the robe and left the room. When she returned to the kitchen, she saw Carmen staring out the window. "It looks horrible out there."

"It will be bad, but nothing we can't overcome," Tricia promised. "Homes can be rebuilt and lives reestablished in time."

With her face drained of color Carmen turned to face Tricia as she realized that her entire life as she knew it was gone and she would be starting over. Tricia took a step toward her and she melted into her arms as the overwhelming realization of what she had survived hit her full force. Sobs shook her frame while her tears wet the front of Tricia's shirt.

"It will be okay," she heard Tricia promise repeatedly as her hands stroked her damp curls. "You are safe and sound and that is all that matters right now. Tomorrow after the storm clears we will ride out and check your property together if that is what you would like."

"I would like that very much. As bad as things were when I left, I am certain it only got worse during the night."

"Is there anyone you need to call? I am not certain, but my cell phone should work."

"I would like to call my sister and check on my staff if that would be all right."

Carmen realized that she knew very little about the woman holding in her arms. However, she was disappointed when Tricia released her and stepped away. "Let me get my phone and you can make calls while I finish breakfast."

"No, I promised you breakfast," Carmen dried her eyes. "I will call after we finish eating."

†

The omelet she made was a superb meal and even Kiki seemed to enjoy bits from the fluffy concoction. Tricia picked up the dishes and handed Carmen the cell phone before disappearing upstairs into the lighthouse to afford her some privacy. As she and Kiki climbed the steps, she could hear her chatting with someone she presumed was her sister and she smiled thankful Carmen was able to make contact with the outside world.

Tricia and Kiki rested against the window frame staring out at the ruined coastline. The dark clouds had mostly passed, but the gloom of destruction lay over the coastline. She could see signs of movement in the distance as survivors began leaving shelters and surveying damages. Probably utility crews and law enforcement she thought as the light rain continued.

The downtown area would surely be flooded and there would be trees and power lines down everywhere, making

125

travel extremely dangerous. A curfew would be in effect at nightfall to protect residents as well as to deter looters who would greedily gobble up the opportunity to benefit from others' misfortune. It was a sad necessity in today's world, but Tricia remained confident that her community would band together to make life more bearable for each other over the next few weeks as the recovery was initiated.

Tricia was facing the west when she heard Carmen climb slowly and carefully up the stairs. She walked next to Tricia and gazed out at the horizon. As brutal as the last twenty-four hours had been, Mother Nature had sent a sunset as beautiful as any they had ever seen. Red, purple, and yellow flames licked the sky as the oversized orange orb slipped beneath the horizon.

"Such a beautiful sight," Carmen said as she stood close.

"Nature never ceases to amaze me." Tricia turned to look at Carmen. "Were you able to make your calls?"

"Yes, thank you. I talked to my sister who wants me to move back to Canada immediately, and to my dental assistant and hygienist who told me that our receptionist evacuated and was safe in Alabama. Everyone took heavy damages, but they and their families are safe."

"Canada, huh? I thought I detected a slight accent."

"Yes, I am from Montreal and moved to Pensacola last year to start a dental practice. No one was able to go by the office yet, so I hope it survived the wrath of the storm."

"If not, I guess I will see what kind of service we receive for paying the hellacious insurance premiums," Tricia said, bringing a smile to Carmen's lips.

Tricia joined her at the windowsill and they gazed in silence out into the fading light. Tricia sighed when the day finally succumbed to darkness. "Would you care for a cup of coffee, or are you ready to lie down?"

"Coffee would be nice." Carmen took the arm offered to her and was slowly led back down the stairs and settled onto the couch.

She brewed a pot of coffee and poured each of them a cup, carrying them into the small living room. Kiki was busily munching the cat chow Tricia had put down for her as she and Carmen sipped the hot brew.

"You make a good cup of coffee and you fixed it just perfect for my tastes."

"Thanks. I hoped that you would like your coffee sweet and light, so I guess I got lucky."

"If anyone here got lucky, I would say it was me. If not for you, I probably wouldn't be sitting here right now. I was just about at the end of my rope when I heard your voice."

"Okay then, we both got lucky. I have to admit, though, I have pulled a lot of fish out of those waters, and even an old tire, but you are by far the prettiest catch I have ever made."

It was Carmen's turn to flush and a rush of color flooded her cheeks. She was speechless and totally enthralled with the woman who had saved her life. *Fate does have a strange way of bringing people together.* Carmen was thankful for the angel sent to her.

They sipped their coffee in comfortable silence. "You look weary. There is probably enough hot water for two quick showers if you want to clean up and put on some fresh clothes before retiring," Tricia said.

"Would there be enough for one long one?"

When she saw the grin on Carmen's face a knot formed in Tricia's throat. "Possibly." *Is this woman really asking me to shower with her?*

"Will you join me, then?" Carmen's question removed any doubt to her intention.

"I would love to." Tricia stood and took her hand, leading her to the small bathroom.

They stripped out of their clothes and stepped under the tepid water, the dark curls of Carmen's hair growing darker in the shower. Tricia picked up the shampoo and slowly massaged the lather into Carmen's hair, leaning her forward under the water long enough to rinse before taking a soft cloth in her hands. She lathered the cloth with a rich smelling soap and slowly and gently bathed Carmen, careful not to press too firmly on the sore ribs and other bruised areas. Rinsing her body and the cloth, Carmen just as gently bathed Tricia and then pulled her under the flow of water to rinse their bodies. Pulling her near brought their lips very close together and when Carmen opened her eyes, she leaned forward and placed her soft lips onto Tricia's.

Her eyes remained closed, as she feared the dream would end if she opened them. Instinctively, she parted her lips and Carmen's tongue slowly entered her mouth for a tender, sensual kiss. The untimely cooling of the water ended the kiss and she reached behind Carmen to shut the water off.

Stepping out of the tub, Tricia selected thick towels for both of them to dry off. Neither of them spoke of the kiss, but she could see a flicker of desire in Carmen's dark eyes when their eyes met again. When they were dry, she took Carmen by the hand and led her into the bedroom.

Carmen took the clothes Tricia had laid out for them on the bed and moved them over to the dresser. "You really don't want those, do you?" Her voice was soft, needy.

"No, I don't." Tricia crawled between the sheets lying on her back, watching as Carmen slipped between the sheets, rolled onto her side, and laid her head on Tricia's shoulders. Silence filled the room as the flames from the candle Tricia had lit earlier danced upon the walls.

Carmen moved her right thigh to rest on top of Tricia as her hand touched the warm skin of her stomach. Her fingertips grazed the skin softly as she slowly made her way up Tricia's body. Tricia felt her nipples swell as Carmen turned her head and velvety lips brushed her neck, kissing her tenderly. Carmen carefully raised herself up to her elbow to allow her lips to once again cover Tricia's and they resumed the kiss started in the shower.

Carmen's hand reached Tricia's left breast, circling the hardened nipple slowly with her nails, causing her to moan deeply as Tricia's hand caressed the soft skin of Carmen's back and hips. She trembled with desire as Carmen's hand slid down her body and between her thighs to gently part the soaked lips and wet her fingertips in the growing moisture. Tricia feared she would pass out from pure pleasure as Carmen's fingers returned to her aching nipples, coating them with her juices.

Breaking the kiss, Carmen whispered, "I want to taste you."

Tricia carefully guided Carmen on top of her, her body screaming out with need as Carmen lowered her mouth onto Tricia's left breast. Carmen sucked her breast as Tricia's hand buried itself in Carmen's hair. Tricia's mind swirled with the pleasure Carmen was giving her while her heart pounded in her chest. She heard Carmen moan loudly as she licked the moisture from Tricia's breasts, hungering for more.

Carmen slid covers from the bed as she slowly kissed her way down Tricia's body until she rested between her open legs. With tender touches, Carmen's fingers parted Tricia's lips as her tongue traced the outline of her opening to begin the most sensual kiss ever imagined. Tricia's body exploded in wave after wave of passion that could rival any storm as Carmen took from her what she needed until Tricia fainted in exhaustion.

When she awoke several minutes later, Carmen was resting on her shoulder watching her closely. Totally spent from the lovemaking, she could barely keep her eyes open, but when she attempted to move Carmen held her still. "Sleep for now, there will be plenty of time later."

Tricia drifted off to sleep, holding onto Carmen, a content smile playing on her face.

The following morning dawned bright and, as they lay snuggled together, Carmen asked, "Are you ready to venture out today?"

"Yes, but there is something else I need to do first." She disappeared beneath the covers.

Consumed

It was the summer of my twenty-seventh year and I was struggling with the development of my fourth novel. I had hit a brick wall with the creation of the book's characters and I had spent endless days writing page after page of worthless text, only to wad them up and toss them in the trash that was now overflowing with debris of dead characters. The walls of my studio home were closing in around me making my writer's block even more dangerous. I knew I had talent, and had successfully published my first three novels in less than two years, but now my agent and publisher were both pressuring me to meet an upcoming deadline for a first draft.

Words used to spring from my head to my computer screen with relative ease before becoming a published author, and it was such a joyful part of my life to tell the stories that grew endlessly in my imagination. Now, with deadlines, book signings, and public relations activities, the pressure to write, to produce a certain number of pages, felt more of a chore than a joy.

It was then that I decided to break away. I asked a friend to house sit while I packed my bags and my laptop and drove north. The Smoky Mountains of western North Carolina have always seemed a second home for me, a place of peace and relaxation, a world apart from the hustle and bustle of the city. It was there in the deep woods that I felt I could find the flow of words that had eluded me, to finish the draft that was due to my agent in three months.

I would escape to the woods where I had spent my summers as a child and later as a college student. I was fortunate to still have family connections in the general area of Asheville and a cousin around my age who had hooked me up with my old summer job. Southwest of Asheville by several hours, there was a vacancy for a firewatcher, someone who could spend endless hours in a fire tower watching for signs of a forest fire. It was here that I had first begun writing during those endless summer hours as a way to pass the time between shifts at the fire tower.

Two persons who would work eight-hour shifts each before being relieved by the oncoming shift would staff each tower. It was far from strenuous work. The most laborious task was climbing the two-hundred-and-four metal steps to reach the top of the observation tower. There were usually two or more high-powered telescopes positioned in the observation post that could pivot around to cover the entire scope of the assigned area. Even with the naked eye, you could see for miles in every direction, and after the morning mist burned off, the sun would illuminate a sea of evergreens.

The local weather station was forecasting a dry summer so the risk of forest fire would be elevated. Careless campers in the area would at times lose control of campfires, or toss a cigarette butt out of a window, and on the rare occasion of a summer thunderstorm, a lightning strike could cause the forest to go up like sticks in a tinderbox. But even though I would need to remain vigilant for signs of fire, there would be plenty of time to spend writing.

I would be sharing a cabin with Morgan Montgomery, a college senior who had spent several summers on the fire watch. Morgan was a major in Forestry Sciences and would work the late daylight hours, the greatest potential time for fires, and I would be responsible for the early morning shift. I wasn't in need of the money. My novels had done well, and I could just as easily have rented or bought a cabin in the woods to do nothing but focus on writing, but the lure of adventure and recapturing a little of my youth spurred me to accept this position.

My Land Rover easily climbed the foothills and wound around the tight curves as I drove through the mountains to Franklin. Surrounded by green I drove through valleys, and dense forest, and even passed an occasional waterfall. When I finally pulled up to the cabin, it was nearly three in the afternoon. The shadows were cooling down for the evening as I unloaded my bags and walked inside.

The cabin was not luxuriantly decorated, or furnished with amenities of today's comfort, but I immediately felt at home with the rustic wooden beams and oversized furniture. I was pleased to see a swing on the front porch, which displayed a panoramic view of a lush valley pasture. Standing there, I could look across to the valley and a hillside dotted with black cattle that were grazing on the rich, tall grasses. The air bathed my lungs with its pureness, the scent of evergreen cleansing the exhaust smoke from my body with every breath.

I located a bedroom that appeared to be vacant and was busy hanging my clothes and emptying my bags into the dresser when I heard the front door open. When I looked out from the closet, a young brunette was standing in the doorway.

"I thought I heard someone pull up. I'm Morgan. You must be Jordan. I have read all of your books and I must say you have a terrific talent." She stepped inside the room. "I nearly fainted when I was told that you would be my partner this summer."

"Well thank you, Morgan," I said rather blandly. "I had this job when I was in college as well and it is where I first began writing. I have run up against a bit of writer's block and I hope that by coming back here I can rejuvenate and get past the block."

"Fantastic. Welcome back and I look forward to getting to know you better, but now I had better get back to work. I have a stew cooking in the crock-pot if you get hungry later, so make yourself at home and I will see you around nine." With that, Morgan was instantly gone.

The aroma of the stew filled the small cabin, making my mouth water. In my rush to escape the city, I had forgotten to eat lunch and the smell of the stew made my stomach growl. I opened the refrigerator, found a large pitcher of cold water, and instinctively reached into the correct cupboard for a glass. I poured a large glass, then dipped out a bowl of the stew, the gravy rich and thick, accompanied by tender meat and fresh garden vegetables. There was a fresh loaf of white bread on the counter and I took a slice to eat with the stew.

The meal was fantastic, simple, but it had a better taste than most gourmet restaurants I had visited in the past few years. I used the bread to soak up the gravy in the bowl and did not waste a drop of the precious liquid. The water, like the mountain air, was pure and tasted totally different from city water or even the best bottled water you could buy, and I drank two glasses with the meal.

After washing up my dishes, I walked outside to the base of the tower and looked up. Two hundred and four steps awaited my feet and I eagerly began my climb. Even my morning jogs did not prepare my muscles for the exertion of the climb. I managed half the steps before I had to stop for a breather. This would definitely take some getting used to again. I was not ancient by any standards, but my legs were not used to climbing this many steps. My lungs, used to the salty air at sea level, burned and I was glad I had given up smoking a few years ago.

I concentrated on the sound of my hiking books on the metal steps. When I stepped inside breathing heavily, Morgan smiled at me. "They take some getting used to."

"Thanks. My legs are already screaming at me, but I wanted to get a good look before the sun went down." I looked out the glass window to find golden rays of sunlight bursting through the clouds to bathe the forest in glowing hues of yellow. The view took my breath away for a moment and I stood there gazing until Morgan broke the silence.

"Is it as beautiful as you remember?"

"Even more than I can remember." I turned to see Morgan smiling at me.

"It has been a relatively quiet fire season so far, but we haven't gotten much rain to help out."

I felt Morgan's eyes watching me as I walked around the observatory.

"I was lucky during my years here to experience only two fires. One caused by a careless Boy Scout campfire and the other sparked by drunken college kids setting off fireworks on the Fourth of July." I smiled remembering back to those carefree days. "We were lucky and neither did much damage."

"I hope we are that lucky this year."

I walked over to the counter near one of the telescopes and saw a large frame of the jigsaw puzzle Morgan had been working on. "I used to love these things." I picked up the box and looked at the picture of the completed puzzle.

"Feel free to do some puzzling with me then. I pick up a couple new ones each week when I go to town for groceries."

"Thanks, I would like that." I looked at my watch, which read four thirty. "I take the morning shift at six, correct?"

"Yes, ma'am, she's all yours from six to two. The Forestry Service still hasn't budgeted a third night watch position, but I assured them we would climb up for a look around regularly if the danger increased or we had a bad storm.

"That sounds good." I stifled a yawn. "I have forgotten what fresh air will do to you."

"I will try to be quiet when I come in later," Morgan said as she walked me to the door.

"Your stew was fantastic by the way." A broad smile was the reward for my compliment.

"I am glad you liked it. Your turn tomorrow night unless you want leftovers." She gave me a wink.

"If it is as good tomorrow as it was today, I would gladly eat it again." I started down the stairway.

"Later." Morgan disappeared back into the tower.

The nearer I came to the bottom of the stairway, the more pronounced the burning in my legs became. When my feet finally touched solid ground, I peered up at the tower and saw Morgan waving at me. *I guess she wanted to make sure I had made it back down in one piece without falling out from a heart attack*, I mused as I waved back and walked back inside the cabin.

136

I stripped out of my travel clothes and walked into the bathroom for a shower. One thing had not changed around the cabin, and that was the limited supply of hot water. There would not be any luxurious twenty-minute showers this summer. I quickly bathed, finishing just as the flow started to cool. I dried off, slipped into a T-shirt and some well-worn boxers, and dropped the dirty clothing back in my room. The cabin had a nice television in the den area and I was surprised to find that cable had arrived in the deep woods of Franklin. During my college days, you had the choice of three local channels, and on many nights, they had been broadcasting the same baseball game, so I was delighted to find many more choices. Ironically, I tuned into a baseball game and settled in on the large couch to watch a few innings.

Those few innings quickly put me to sleep and I napped on the couch until I heard the door open and raised my head to see Morgan walking in.

"The couch took you prisoner I see," Morgan said, noting the sleep still evident in my eyes.

"I was just going to watch a few innings of a ball game and I must have drifted off."

"This place has an enchanting way of putting you to sleep if you remain in one position too long." Morgan grinned.

"I see that now." I sat up on the couch still rubbing my eyes.

"I am going to shower quickly and eat dinner if you would care to join me," Morgan casually mentioned.

"For the shower or the meal," I said without thinking.

"Both if you would like," Morgan came back without missing a beat, smiling as my face turned scarlet.

"I am sorry, that just slipped out," I stammered in my embarrassment. I really didn't even know where that thought came from, but it was obviously floating around in my brain.

"Not a problem," Morgan chuckled. "There are fresh strawberries in the fridge. If you wash and slice them I will make shortcakes for dessert." She disappeared into the bathroom, not waiting for my reply.

I walked over to the fridge, located the strawberries, washed them under cool water in the kitchen sink, and was busy slicing them when Morgan returned from the shower. She was also dressed in a T-shirt and boxers and went to work dipping out a bowl of stew. "Would you care for more?"

"No, I think strawberry shortcake and a glass of milk will hold me until the morning." I finished slicing the berries, carried them to the table, and sat down while Morgan finished preparing her meal. When she walked over to the table and sat down, the fabric of her boxers rode up her thigh revealing a wicked red burn scar. As hard as I tried not to stare, I could not keep my eyes off the mark that ran fully across her left thigh.

Morgan reached down to cover her damaged skin with the soft fabric of the boxers, concealing the scar from view. It was obvious the scar was emotionally painful to Morgan and I wanted to kick myself. In the last hour alone, I had managed to embarrass myself twice and cause an innocent young woman discomfort. My actions were so unusual for me I started to worry if I had made a good decision in coming to this place.

"I am sorry for staring," I stammered in attempt to apologize.

"No problem, I am slowly getting used to the shocked looks."

138

"Still, Morgan, I have been here less than twenty-four hours and I have made you uncomfortable twice now."

"Not at all. I was quite amused by your shower comment, and the scar, well, it is something I have to deal with."

"Since I am on a downward spiral here, can I ask what happened?"

Morgan swallowed the bite of stew and washed it down with a drink of water. "Last summer I was chosen to train in Colorado as a fire jumper, a firefighter who is airlifted above the fire to rappel down onto the ground in an effort to slow the progress of a fire." She picked up a slice of the bread and dipped it in the stew's gravy as she talked. "I was two weeks from graduating at the top of the class when a fire broke out on the mountain and we were sent up to prevent the fire's spread onto a nearby cattle ranch."

She took a bite of her stew and chewed as she carefully planned her next words. "We were battling the fire and had it almost contained when the winds whipped up and we were suddenly surrounded by walls of flames."

I could feel myself on the edge of my seat as I leaned forward, engrossed by her story.

"Two of my fellow classmates were victims of the smoke and the surging flames. While I was awaiting evacuation from the site, a small tree collapsed and pinned me to the ground. Two of my instructors were able to cut and lift the tree off my leg, but not before it had burned through my protective suit, and the impact had fractured my femur."

Morgan remained quiet for a few minutes and I noticed that her hand had unconsciously moved to rub across the bright scar. "After surgery to pin my leg, and two skin grafts to date, I am left with this ugly reminder. I still have several more grafts to undergo, but the most painful part, other than losing two classmates, is that it prevents me from ever being a fire jumper. The scar tissue will always be very sensitive, especially to heat, and the damage to my femur would also prevent me from receiving a medical clearance to jump."

"I am so sorry, Morgan. That must have been a terrifying experience."

"It was, but I was lucky to have survived, and I will still have a career with the Forestry Service after I graduate next spring." She gave me a weak smile. "So, enough about me for now, tell me something about you." Morgan resumed eating her meal.

"Well, you already know I am a writer and my fourth novel is due out by the beginning of next year, but I have hit a wall with the story. I hope some fresh air and less stress will allow me to resume the writing that I once loved so much."

"This place is perfect for de-stressing, Jordan. As long as you don't get sick of me, there will be no one else around to put pressure on you. I think by now you have discovered that cell phones don't work in this area, so mine is the only voice you will hear unless you go into town." Morgan gave me a wink and a grin.

"I think I can handle that, if you can tolerate me." I returned a bashful smile.

"Only on one condition," Morgan said, surprising me with the comment.

"And that would be?"

"That you can make good coffee because, frankly, mine sucks." She was very serious for a second and then broke into laughter.

"That I can do." I joined the infectious laughter.

"It's a done deal then. Are you ready for dessert?" She stood and walked to the pantry.

"All this laughter has made me hungry. Can I help with anything?"

"You already have sliced the strawberries so all I need is the angel food cake and some cool whip which you can get from the fridge while you pour your milk." Morgan cut two large slices from the cake and placed them in bowls. Then she took a fork and mashed up the strawberry slices, creating juice from the ripe berries, and sprinkled a spoonful of sugar on top before dipping out the sweet concoction to cover the cake.

"That looks delicious." I watched Morgan place one of the bowls in front of me.

"Dig in." She joined me at the table with her own bowl.

Over the next hour we engaged in harmless chat, both sharing the rather bland facts of our lives as we finished off the dessert and cleaned the kitchen together. It was getting late and my alarm would be going off at five the next morning, so I told Morgan goodnight and thanked her for the great dessert.

"I need to unwind some still, so would you mind if I turned the television on?"

"Not at all. I will be out like a light as soon as my head hits the pillow."

"Goodnight then," I heard Morgan say as I walked to the bedroom.

Checking the alarm, I made certain it was set, and then crawled between the crisp, fresh sheets. For a moment, I listened for the soft hum of the television before drifting off to sleep.

†

I awoke the next morning at a quarter to five and reached over to silence the alarm. It was not unusual for my internal clock to go off before my alarm, and I was thankful that the noise would not be waking Morgan. I sat up on the edge of the bed and searched for my slippers. The room was cool and I knew the floor would be as well. I slipped my feet into my soft lambskin slippers and walked to the kitchen to start the coffee. I opened the refrigerator and found a bagel, sliced it, and dropped it in the toaster. I poured a glass of apple juice and placed it on the table as the bagel was toasting. The coffee was brewing, filling the room with a heady aroma. When the bagel popped up from the toaster, I placed it on a small saucer, carried it to the table where I spread cream cheese across the top of it, and then walked back to pour a cup of coffee. I sat at the table and ate my meal in the peaceful quiet of the morning.

I noticed a small notepad on the desk and after I had finished eating, I wrote *Good Morning Sunshine* on a page and placed the notepad by the coffee pot where Morgan would be sure to see. I don't know what had overcome me, but I felt an intoxicating need to flirt with her. Talking with her and hearing her laughter made me feel giddy and I realized just how lonesome I had grown. I had poured my second cup of coffee, and was standing in front of the coffee pot when I heard moans coming from Morgan's room. The sound was eerie. I took my coffee and walked to her bedroom door.

The moans grew louder as I approached. I stopped at the door to her room and looked in. Morgan was still asleep and, from the way she writhed in the bed, I suspected she was having a bad dream. Her moans sounded like she was in pain, but it was difficult to tell if they were real or just part of her dream. I listened and could make out the name "Meagan" as I watched tears stream down Morgan's cheeks. I contemplated waking her, then thought better of my decision, and left her to finish her dream. I dressed quickly and quietly brushed my teeth and hair before stepping out into a cool morning.

The namesake mist of the Smokey's hung thick and shrouded the tower. Standing at the base and looking up, I could only see half of the metal steps that disappeared into the haze. There wouldn't be much to see, but I should be able to get some writing done before the mist burnt off and the sun illuminated the beautiful mountains. I shouldered my laptop bag and started the climb, silently counting each of the steps. The muscles of my legs felt tight and stiff as each step echoed in the cool morning air.

I refused to allow myself to stop, forcing my legs all the way to the top. I was breathing deeply by the time I reached the top and surprised to find I had broken a light sweat in the coolness. I reached for the handle that was cold in my hand and I wished I had remembered a jacket or sweatshirt. When I opened the door, the warmth that greeted me surprised me. In the center of the room, a small heater poured out electric warmth and filled the room with a soft glow.

I smiled as I walked over to the counter and placed my laptop bag on its surface. On a notepad by the lamp was a handwritten note from Morgan.

Welcome Home! I hope you have a fantastic first day back in the tower. I will bring lunch up around noon. I hope you like egg salad ;-)
M

Egg salad was one of my favorite sandwiches, but there was no way Morgan could have known that. There was something special about that woman and it stirred desires that I hadn't felt in ages. Those feelings both terrified and excited me as I began my first morning in the tower.

I eagerly set up my laptop and within minutes the words began to flow, and it felt...good. Thirty more minutes had expired before I looked up from the keyboard to see that the sun was beginning to burn through the mist and light the forest. I stood and took a walk around the observatory. Most of the woods were still shrouded in the haze, but where the sun's rays were burning through the leaves, it coated them in a golden hue.

I stopped in front of the counter that held the jigsaw puzzle and could not resist picking a piece and turning it in my fingers until my eye located the spot where it fit perfectly. My fingers snapped it in place. I walked over to where I had been sitting at the laptop and pressed the button on a small timer that began a countdown from thirty minutes. Then I walked back to the puzzle and looked at the cover again that showed a beautiful picture of the Stone Arches of Moab, Utah. I sat down in the chair where I presumed Morgan had spent countless hours and began to puzzle.

Startled by the sound of the timer going off, I hadn't realized I'd been concentrating on the puzzle so intensely that I had lost track of the passing of time. I stood and made rounds, noting the sun was lighting over half the valley as the shadows were slowly disappearing.

The flashing of the cursor brought my attention back to the laptop and, after setting the timer, I sat down and began typing again. I spent the remainder of the morning composing the first chapter of my novel and was busy proofreading when I heard the rhythmic thump, thump of Morgan's boots as she climbed the stairs to the tower. As her steps grew louder, I stood and walked to the door to meet her.

"Hello," Morgan said as she looked up and saw me waiting for her.

"Can I help with anything?"

"No, Jordan, I have it under control."

"Egg salad is my favorite." My mouth began watering for the taste.

"I made a good choice then," Morgan said as she reached the top. "I hope you like sweet baby gherkins, too."

"And a pitcher of sweet tea? My lord, I have died and gone to heaven."

"It's the least I could do in appreciation for finally getting a decent cup of coffee this morning."

"I will make you coffee every morning, then."

"I couldn't ask for a better deal." She walked to the counter and sat the tray down.

She took the plastic wrap off a stack of sandwiches cut in half and popped the lid on the pickle jar as I poured two glasses of tea. Morgan glanced over at the laptop.

"Having any luck with the writing?"

"Not bad so far." I sat next to her, bit into a sandwich, and moaned in appreciation.

"Now, that sound is heaven to my ears." Morgan grinned.

I thought of the moans coming from Morgan's room earlier this morning, but did not think it was a good time to mention them.

"This is the best egg salad I have ever eaten." I finished off the first half of a sandwich, and grabbed for another.

"I am glad you are enjoying it."

"I took some pork chops out of the freezer this morning. I thought I would bake them with some macaroni and cheese and fresh green beans, if that's good with you."

"That sounds fantastic, Jordan."

I noticed Morgan was rubbing her thigh as she ate. "Are you hurting today?"

"We are going to get rain in the next few days. Since the accident, I always know when it is coming."

"Maybe you should consider a career in weather forecasting". I grinned.

"That might not be a bad idea at all," Morgan said, returning my grin. "The dull ache I get is much more reliable and accurate than most of the forecasts you see on the television. I can guarantee that we will have rain within the next two days."

"I hope you are correct, we sure could use it. I don't know about you, but I love a nice gentle rain, especially at night on the tin roof of the cabin, makes me sleep like a baby."

"I could use a good night's sleep," Morgan said.

"You have trouble sleeping?"

"I couldn't tell you when I last had a full night of sleep. Why are you blushing?"

"When I was drinking coffee this morning, I heard you moaning and when I went to look in on you. You appeared to be dreaming, clutching your pillow, and you called out a name."

"Meagan?"

I blushed again and nodded.

Morgan was silent for several minutes before she looked me in the eyes. Her green eyes that normally sparkled so bright were full of tears. "Meagan and I were lovers for two years. She was one of the two fire jumpers who were killed on the mountain that day." Tears were rolling down her cheeks.

"We were running up the mountain to the evacuation point when she collapsed from smoke inhalation and as I turned to help her onto her feet, the tree fell pinning us both to the hot ground." Morgan stood and walked across the room. She looked out the window and took a deep breath before she continued the story. "Our instructors returned to attempt a rescue, using chainsaws to cut the tree off us, but it was too late for Meagan." Morgan broke down in sobs. "She died in my arms."

I stood up, walked over to Morgan, wrapped my arms around her, and held her close. Her body wracked with hard sobs as she mourned her lost love. We rocked together slowly until she was able to control her tears and she looked up to me with bloodshot eyes. "Thank you."

I leaned down, kissed the top of her head, and hugged her close.

"I needed to get that out of my system. Almost every night I dream of her and until now, no one ever knew that she and I were lovers."

I stepped back from her and looked her directly in her eyes. "Thank you for sharing that with me. That gives me perspective on how you felt about Meagan and the tremendous loss you have experienced."

"It was the most difficult time of my life. My injury prevented me from attending her funeral and I feel like I have no sense of closure. My mind just will not let her go." She began to cry again.

I reached out to her and she stepped into my arms, pulling me close, clinging to me desperately as she purged the tears she had held in for so long. I had no words to comfort her, and I felt completely inadequate to help Morgan deal with her grief, so I just held onto her for dear life.

Morgan cried until she had no tears left. When she stepped back, she seemed different, a little more relaxed, and there seemed to be a different sparkle in her eyes. She looked at me, cocked her head to the side, and smiled at me. No words passed between us, just that look and that smile, and I felt my heart melting. I desperately wanted to take Morgan into my arms and kiss her at that moment, but I would not take advantage of her vulnerability. If we were to share a kiss, Morgan needed to initiate it when she felt the time was right for her to move on.

As if sensing my interest, Morgan turned back to the table. "I guess I had better get moving if I am going to be relieving you at two." Morgan picked up the tray and before I could think of any words to speak, she was out the door and moving quickly down the steps.

I sighed, confused about what had just transpired between us, and spent the remainder of my shift trying to sort out my scattered thoughts. I looked at the computer and sat down in front of it, opening up a new file and started typing what I was feeling, my fingers flying across the keys with a will of their own. I don't remember thinking the words that came to life on the computer's screen and when my thoughts were finished I scrolled back to the top and began reading. When I got to the bottom of the third and final page, my thoughts were crystal clear. I was about to type the final three words when I heard Morgan come rushing up the stairs. I quickly saved the file and shut down the computer, suddenly embarrassed by the thoughts I was having, and closed the computer lid just as Morgan came through the door.

"Welcome back."

She walked directly over to me and hugged me close. I could smell the fragrance of the shampoo in her hair, still damp from the shower. I felt a shiver run through me, even though my blood was on fire.

"Are you cold?"

"Just a quick shiver." I quickly turned away. "See you at nine?"

"My mouth is already watering for pork chops."

I felt Morgan watch me walk toward the door. "I will have dinner ready when you get home." I slipped out the door and made my way down the steps.

The warm sunshine felt marvelous on my skin as I descended from the tower. The day had blossomed into a beautiful afternoon, and reluctant to return inside, I decided to walk down the lane to the mailbox even though I doubted there would be any mail inside. I was halfway down the lane when I heard movement in the bushes to my right. I froze in my tracks and waited until a pair of chipmunks came scurrying across my path, stopping to give me a once-over before chattering to each other and disappearing into bushes on the other side of the lane.

When I reached the end of the lane, I looked down the desolate blacktop and found it empty in both directions. Along the rarely used road, the only sounds carried through the air were the calling of birds and the bellowing of a cow in search of a wayward calf. Life seemed so simple, the air sweet and clean, and my heart was lost to the woman making rounds in the observatory several hundred yards away. How was I to proceed, I wondered as I removed the junk mail and walked slowly back to the cabin.

I looked into the refrigerator and the pork chops had fully thawed, so I placed them in the refrigerator and walked toward my room. I decided that a shower and nap were in order before starting dinner, so I stripped off my clothes and walked to the bathroom. The shower was very relaxing and when I had dried, I was ready for a nap. I didn't bother with clothing and stretched out on top of the bed. Looking out the window, I could see the top of the tower and I wondered what Morgan was doing. The way her green eyes sparkled at me made me smile and I found my hands softly stroking my skin as I closed my eyes and imagined Morgan's hands caressing me. My nipples grew hard as my fingertips circled them slowly and I felt my body responding, moisture growing between my thighs.

It had been over a year since I had allowed myself to feel the pleasure that was coursing through my veins now and my body was eagerly responding to the attention. My hands caressed further down, stroking the inside of my thighs as a climax began to build in the core of my being. The fingertips of my left hand gently parted my lips, and I could feel my clit as it continued to swell with excitement, engorged with blood.

As I glanced out the window, I saw Morgan peering down at the cabin, and I knew she had a clear view into my room and saw me lying naked on the bed. The thought of Morgan watching made my heart pound as my hands teased and stimulated my body. I smiled, hoping she was enjoying the show hips rocking to a sensual rhythm as my fingers slid in and out of my body.

I shook with delight as my fingers delved deeper with each thrust of my hips. My breath caught in my throat as the first wave of orgasm passed and continued for several minutes.

My eyes closed briefly as I climaxed and the room filled with soft moans of the pleasure I was experiencing. I was disappointed when my eyes reopened, to find that Morgan had moved away from the window.

My body relaxed in complete satisfaction and I quickly drifted into slumber, still lying naked on the bed. I slept for two hours, then ran back through the shower before dressing and starting dinner. I placed the pork chops in the oven to allow them to bake slowly and went to the den to watch some television. I would start the rest of the meal at eight and have everything piping hot when Morgan came down from the tower.

†

I was placing the last of the dishes on the table when I heard Morgan's boots on the porch, and a few seconds later she walked through the door. Her eyes lit up at the table full of food and she rewarded me with a brilliant smile.

"My, that sure does look good. Let me go wash up and I will be right back." Morgan slipped into the bathroom to wash her hands.

I poured two glasses of tea and sat at the table when she returned. "Dig in," I said as she took a seat.

We ate the meal over light conversation and when she could eat no more, Morgan pushed her chair back from the table. "I will explode if I eat another bite."

"You better stop then."

"If you plan on cooking like this every night, I better find my running shoes and take up jogging again."

The image of a hot and sweaty Morgan flashed before my eyes and I felt my face go hot. She noticed and gave me a curious look, but did not comment. "Why don't you take a shower and I will do the dishes," I suggested.

"You have a deal, Jordan, if you are sure I can't help."

"I have most of them done already, so it won't take but a minute"

"I will be back soon then." Morgan stated as she left the room.

I finished cleaning the kitchen, walked back to the den, and lay down on the couch to watch the movie playing on the screen while Morgan finished showering. When she walked into the room and sat on the edge of the couch, I moved to sit up and she reached out to stop me.

"Stay where you are."

"No, I need to quit hogging the couch."

"Well, I was hoping that you would hold me again?"

I smiled and moved backwards on the couch and rolled onto my side. "Join me?"

Morgan shifted and lay down beside me facing the television and scooting next to me, placing her head on my outstretched arm under the pillow. I wrapped my left arm around her waist and held her close. The smell of her clean hair and the warmth of her body next to mine was pure torture. I lay my head next to hers and breathed in her scent as I pretended to watch the movie. We lay there in silence, sharing the comfort of one another until the movie ended.

Morgan turned the television off, rolled over on the couch, and lay facing me. Our lips were mere inches apart. My tongue snaked out to wet my lips and Morgan smiled softly. She leaned forward and closed her eyes as our lips met, softly brushing in a tender kiss. The kiss lasted for only a few seconds before Morgan reached up to stroke my cheek.

"Sleep with me tonight. No expectations, but I could use your comfort."

I nodded. Morgan stood, taking my hand to lead me into her bedroom. She pulled back the covers, climbed into the bed, and reached for my hand again to pull me in close behind her. I snuggled close to her and pulled the covers over us. I wrapped my arm around her waist and this time she took my hand in hers holding it gently.

My body was soaring with desire as we lay so close in the bed, but I was content in holding Morgan close. I was about to whisper goodnight when I heard her softly purring as she slept. With a smile frozen on my face, I held her while she slept and the comfortable warmth of her body enticed me to join her in sleep.

Around three in the morning, I awoke, still wrapped around Morgan. I could see the soft smile playing on her face as she slept and my ears picked up a faint sound coming from outside. I looked at the window to discover small rivers of raindrops sliding down the glass panes. The raindrops reminded me of the tears Morgan had shed that day and her promise of a coming rain. Her prediction was correct and I listened to the rain gently pelting the tin roof with a smile gracing my face.

I felt Morgan shift her body and when I looked back from the window, she was watching me. "I told you so," she softly whispered.

"I never doubted you for a second."

Morgan moved closer to me, our bodies touching, and she lifted her hand to softly stroke my face. Her fingers felt so soft against my skin and her touch made my body tingle with excitement. Her eyes searched mine, looking for an answer to an unspoken question, the silence hanging in the air between us.

"Jordan," she whispered, calling my name.

I leaned down and brushed her lips with mine, a soft kiss that lingered only briefly as I raised my head to look into her eyes. Her eyes were glowing like emeralds as she pulled my head back down for another kiss. Morgan's tongue penetrated my lips, gently sliding into my mouth, and I could taste the sweetness of her tongue as it swirled slowly inside. She rolled me onto my back as the kiss grew deeper. When she draped her left leg over my thigh and rested part of her weight on me, I was consumed by her passion.

The heat between us soared like the flames of a forest fire, her kiss stealing the oxygen from my lungs, fueling the desire between us. My hand slid beneath her shirt, fingertips slowly dragging up her spine. Her left hand found my right breast, teasing my nipple through the fabric of my shirt and I arched my back eager for her touch. I ached to feel Morgan's skin so I slowly worked the shirt up her back until she broke our kiss and pulled it over her head, tossing it to the floor. She raised my shirt and removed it, devouring my body with her bright eyes before leaning down to continue the kiss. Her skin was hot on my body as her fire burned into me, igniting an uncontrollable lust in me.

I pulled her body fully on top of me, my hands tugging at her hips as I ground into her. Moans filled the room, I could not separate mine from hers, our mouths and bodies locked together in a sensual dance, oblivious to anything but the need between us. Her hands had covered my breasts, kneading them as her hips rolled rhythmically between my drenched thighs.

My hands caressed her from hips to breasts, the soft flesh hot to my touch. Her nipples were hard and my mouth ached to kiss them. With an aggressive move, I rolled Morgan onto her back and covered her body with mine as I began to lick and kiss my way down her neck, rolling her nipples between my fingers. This time I was certain it was Morgan's moans that filled the room. Her eyes watched intently as my mouth inched its way down to her right breast. I flicked my tongue out to lightly brush across her nipple and Morgan reached out to bury her hand in my hair as she pulled my mouth down onto her breast. I could feel her dampness soak through her boxers as I feasted on her breast. My teeth raked over her nipple as my right hand worked on removing Morgan's boxers, sliding them down as she raised her hips and helped me take them from her body. I removed my boxers and we were completely skin to skin.

Morgan's nails trailed up and down my back as I sucked her breast. I could feel her juices, silky and hot against my skin, and I knew I had to taste her soon or I would explode. My fingers crept between her thighs, bathing in the drops of moisture covering her soft curls. I could feel her clit as it peeked out from its protective cover, hot to the touch and begging for attention.

Unable to restrain myself further, I moved down the bed until I rested between Morgan's legs, the width of my shoulders spreading her thighs. My fingers opened her and my tongue traced the ridges of her lips, and her sweet taste erupted in my mouth. It was my turn to moan loudly. I soared with excitement as I drank from what Morgan offered.

Her fingers clutched the sheets as my tongue slipped inside her, delving deep inside her as I lapped up her juices. My tongue swirled and caressed as my thumb slowly circled her throbbing clit until she cried out and arched her hips, filling my mouth with a rush of liquid heaven. Two of my fingers penetrated her deeply as my mouth closed over her clit, sucking it against the roof of my mouth, and I loved her slowly until she shuddered and came again. The inner walls of her muscles constricted around my fingers as spasms pulsed through her. I softly kissed her clit and gently removed my fingers as she lay gasping for breath.

I lay my head on her thigh as I tried to regain my breath as well, my fingers reaching over to touch the angry red skin of her scar. Morgan reached over to pull the sheet over her thigh to hide the damaged flesh and I gently, but firmly pushed her hand aside. My fingers traced the contours of her skin and I softly kissed the raised surface of the scar that caused her so much pain.

I looked up to find Morgan looking at me, tears trailing down her cheeks like the raindrops sliding down the window panes. I climbed back up to lie beside her and folded her into my arms, holding her close as she wept.

She rested her head on my shoulder and I could feel the pounding of her heart in her chest. My hand softly stroked her hair as her tears continued to fall. When Morgan's tears abated, she raised her head from my shoulder to speak, but I placed a finger to her lips.

"Shh, not now. Just relax and listen."

We lay there, wrapped around one another, listening to the gently falling rain until sleep captured us again. I woke a few hours later and crept from the bed to start the coffee. When I was finished, I crawled back in bed to snuggle Morgan awake.

So began our summer. The love we shared flourished, growing every day. My novel sprang to life in the fire tower and the draft was finished in record time. I knew this one would be my best so far when we drove to town together to mail it off to my editor. I had indeed rejuvenated my writing, but more importantly, I had found a love like no other, one that consumed my heart, and when the summer ended I sold my home in the city and bought a beautiful cabin near a mountaintop. My love returned to school and by the spring, she had graduated and was now my Ranger Montgomery.

Morgan had one more skin graft on her leg and then was content that she would carry the remainder of the damage for life. The red, distorted skin would serve as a constant reminder of her strength and courage and the love she had shared with Meagan.

Sometimes on hot summer nights, we still ride out to the fire tower and climb to the top to sit and gaze out at the stars gracing the night sky as we reminisce back to the first summer we shared together.

Four years and six novels later, we continue to live happily together.

Shooting Stars

The night air was cool and Jess was glad that she and Lauren had chosen heavy coats to wear that evening. Jess was leaning back against the cab of her old work truck with Lauren tucked between her legs, her head resting against Jess's shoulder. The alarm on Lauren's wrist beeped to notify them that a new hour had begun and their eyes began to search the skies.

†

One in the morning marked the estimated beginning of tonight's Leonid meteor shower and, with her arms wrapped around Lauren, Jess gazed toward the heavens. They searched for the first blaze of light across the sky as a comfortable silence surrounded them.

Jess thought back to a similar night, five years earlier. It was the summer of their junior year in college and Lauren had agreed to spend a long weekend at Jess's family cabin by the lake. They had been best friends since high school and roommates in college. They were nearly inseparable and shared a great love for one another as friends.

It had been a miserably hot day and they had cooled off by swimming in the lake until late in the afternoon. When they crawled upon the floating dock thirty yards off shore, they collapsed on their backs giggling. Jess could not remember now what had been so funny, but she did remember the way Lauren's blue eyes sparkled when she laughed. Darkness was falling fast, but neither of them made an effort to move from the dock. Their bodies pressed close and Lauren moved closer to place her head on Jess's shoulder as they watched the night sky come to life. Lauren frequently curled up close to Jess whenever they watched television or movies together and they enjoyed the comfort of one another.

This time it felt different to Jess for reasons she could not quite fathom. The feeling of Lauren so close to her made her tingle. Jess enjoyed the clean smell of Lauren's hair as her head lay on her shoulder, and the way Lauren's body vibrated against hers when she laughed. Lauren's right hand rested comfortably on Jess's left thigh as she pointed out stars in their constellations to Jess. Jess was lost in thought, struggling against the desire she felt building for her friend when Lauren suddenly giggled and shouted, "Shooting star, make a wish, Jess."

Jess closed her eyes and made her wish. Lauren rolled over onto her side, facing Jess. "So, what did you wish for?"

"I can't tell you or it won't come true."

Lauren fixed her blues eyes on Jess and pouted. "You can tell me."

Jess swallowed hard. If she told her friend what her wish was she could ruin the best friendship she had ever had, but she knew Lauren would know if she made up a story.

"Do you really want to know?" Jess met Lauren's gaze.

Lauren reached up and did something she had never done before. She let her fingers trace down Jess's jaw line and Jess felt her body shiver from the gentle touch.

"Yes, I do," Lauren said, with a beautiful smile.

Jess breathed in deeply and then exhaled slowly. "I wished that I could kiss you." She held her breath again while waiting for a response from Lauren.

"I have been waiting for that for over a year now. Yes, you may kiss me, Jess."

Jess's head was spinning with emotion. Did her best friend really just say she wanted a kiss? Her heart was racing in her chest as Jess realized that Lauren was admitting to having special feelings for her and she felt paralyzed with fear.

"Well," Lauren waited.

The softness in her voice melted away Jess's fear and she rolled onto her side to face Lauren. In what felt like super slow motion, Jess closed her eyes and leaned forward until her lips pressed against Lauren's. The smooth, wet lips that touched hers ignited a passion in Lauren and she parted her lips to allow her tongue to softly lick Jess's lips, until they parted and her tongue slipped inside Jess's mouth. Jess moaned loudly and the vibrations in her mouth added to the sensuality of the kiss as their tongues entwined in bliss.

Lauren's hands pulled Jess on top of her as their tongues continued to explore one another's mouths. Jess had never felt anything like the kiss they were sharing and the feeling of Lauren's hard nipples pressed against her sparked a hunger in her that she had never known. Lauren's hands moved down to Jess's hips and she cupped the cheeks of her ass with her hands as she began to slowly grind her hips into Jess. Startled by the surge of moisture between her thighs

159

caused by the movement of Lauren against her, Jess felt an ache ignited deep inside her. Her hips matched the rhythm of Lauren's while their kisses grew more heated.

They broke their kiss, gasping for air, and Lauren breathlessly whispered, "Make love to me, Jess."

Fingers trembling with desire and trepidation, Jess reached up and lowered the straps of Lauren's bathing suit as she rose to her knees to pull the suit down Lauren's body. Jess's heart pounded in her ears as Lauren lifted her hips to allow her to remove the suit completely. Jess had seen Lauren naked many times over the years of their friendship, but she had never looked as beautiful as she did at that moment. She gazed in awe of Lauren's body, her erect nipples swelling with each breath. The closely trimmed patch of dark curls that lined her lower lips glowed with the dampness of her desire.

"I want to feel your skin on mine," Lauren said as she gazed into Jess's eyes.

She watched as Jess removed her suit, revealing her swollen nipples and her eyes seemed to follow Jess's hands as they slid her suit off.

Lauren reached out to Jess and pulled her down on top of her as their mouths locked again.

Jess covered Lauren with her warmth as their skin touched and swollen nipples grazed one another as their bodies melted together. Jess was pressed between Lauren's thighs, and as their bodies moved, their wetness blended together, clit against throbbing clit.

Lauren's hands moved urgently on Jess's body, pressing her shoulders, which encouraged Jess to move her kisses farther south. Jess buried her face in Lauren's neck, breathing in the smell of her as her lips grazed softly up to her chin. Lauren's body burned with need and she took Jess's head in her hands and pressed it down to her right breast.

Jess's hands gently cupped the curves of Lauren's full breasts and gave them a gentle squeeze. Lauren writhed beneath Jess, coating her belly with the liquid silkiness of her excitement as Jess teased her sensitive nipples with her fingers. Her moans of pleasure echoed across the quiet lake as Jess bent her head and took a breast in her mouth, sucking the soft flesh as her tongue rolled the stiff nipple against the roof of her mouth.

Lauren's hands slid between them to cover Jess's smaller breasts, and she tugged and rolled her nipples as Jess sucked harder on her breast. "Oh yes, baby," Lauren breathed as Jess's teeth grazed her nipple and then moved her mouth to administer sweet attention to her other breast.

Lauren's hands on her breasts were driving Jess wild with desire as she fought back the climax she felt building. Eager to taste Lauren, Jess kissed her way down Lauren's belly until she rested completely between her trembling thighs. Lauren was gasping for breath as Jess used her fingertips to part Lauren's shiny lips. Using the tip of her tongue, Jess tasted the sweetness of Lauren for the first time, and her tongue circled her throbbing clit. Lauren's hips bucked against Jess's tongue as she begged to have Jess's tongue inside her. Jess licked down the length of Lauren's lips and, as she began licking upward, she entered Lauren, her tongue deeply exploring her velvety wetness.

Lauren shivered violently as her climax overwhelmed her attempted restraint and her hands held Jess in place as the explosion of her excitement flowed into Jess's waiting mouth. The taste of Lauren sent Jess reeling as she joined Lauren in orgasm and they lie panting breathlessly on the floating dock.

Lauren opened her arms and enveloped Jess in a loving embrace as her best friend and now lover climbed into her arms. Their tongues danced in jubilant celebration as they shared the taste of their lovemaking. For hours that night, they kissed and fondled one another until the full moon rose, and then they agreed to swim to shore to continue exploring their newly found love in the large comfortable bed. They had spent the remainder of the weekend, tucked cozily inside the cabin and their love had blossomed into the relationship they continued to cherish five years later.

†

Jess was startled from her dream as Lauren squealed and pointed off to the east as a shower of falling stars exploded across the dark night sky. Lauren turned her body to face Jess and smiled as she said, "Make a wish, baby."

Jess closed her eyes and made that wish and when she opened her eyes again, Lauren's eyes sparkled down at her.

"What did you wish for?" Lauren asked.

"I wished that the beautiful woman in my arms tonight would be forever mine." With tears glistening in her eyes, Lauren leaned forward and kissed Jess softly on the lips.

"Wish granted." Lauren snuggled into Jess and they watched the night sky until the morning light arrived.

All In

Kristen cursed her luck as the rental car coughed and then coasted to the side of the road, the radiator obviously ruptured as steam hissed wickedly from underneath the hood. She had barely made it seven hours from her broken home when the Rent-a-Wreck breathed its last breath and left her stranded on the interstate.

Her plan up to this point had proceeded smoothly, *almost too smoothly*, she thought as she took mental inventory of the possessions tossed quickly into the back seat as she fled her life in south Florida. A duffle bag was stuffed with enough clothing to last her for several days and her backpack held a sizeable amount of cash, cleaned out from the joint account she managed for herself and her husband, John, and several fake IDs and passports. She had used one of the fake IDs and paid cash for the rambling car she hoped would get her safely to her planned destination.

Earlier that afternoon she had parked their Cadillac in a remote parking garage at the Miami airport and hoped that, along with the fact she had purchased a plane ticket for

Amsterdam, would give her a few days' lead into her new life as a fugitive from justice.

"Justice, such an ironic word," she hissed out loud. *Where was the justice when the beatings occurred over the last four years?* John's Sheriff Department brother, who conveniently made assault charges disappear to protect his older sibling, swept that justice under the carpet. He camouflaged the repeated emergency visits for broken bones and lacerations with elaborate stories of substance abuse, and he threatened incarceration in a mental health facility.

One bit of fortune was smiling down on her. She was looking out the passenger side window, down an incline which led into a small copse of dense trees. With relative ease, she pushed the car over the edge and guided it into the trees, hiding it from easy detection. She carefully wiped down the steering wheel and interior of the car after she had removed her two bags, and then locked the car to add one final deterrent to early detection of her ruse.

Taking the nine millimeter and tucking it into the waistband of her jeans, and concealed under her jacket, she bent down to sling the smaller backpack over her shoulder. Then she picked up the duffle as she continued her trek northward. A few more miles and she would reach the junction of Interstate 10. Her journey west would begin.

Darkness fell quickly and her dark clothing helped to conceal her from passing law enforcement officials. She prayed for a few days' lead before her crime became evident and the hunt for her would begin. By that time, she hoped to be safely across the border and heading deep into Mexico where she could begin a new chapter of her life.

As she briskly walked into the moonless night, she thought back over the events of the past few weeks. Unable to withstand anymore of John's physical and emotional abuse, she had begun to formulate a plan. It was now or never. She had to go all in with her plan or she wouldn't survive much longer. She slowly began making withdrawals from the bank accounts until she had them cleaned out. She had also maxed out the cash advances on the numerous credit cards they shared to give her the highest possible bankroll of cash so she could start her new life. Two hundred thousand didn't seem like much in the States, but in Mexico, she could live like a queen for quite some time. Kristen had already made plans to purchase a small villa deep in Mexico and would finalize the purchase as soon as she reached her destination.

She told their friends that she and John were going out of town on a short trip so no one would worry if they weren't visible for a few days. She even called to stop the paper delivery and had the post office hold mail service to further add to her ruse.

She carefully planned and packed for her escape and put the final phase in place earlier that morning. The unhealed bruises on her face from the last beating were turning yellow as she spiked John's morning coffee with several of her pain pills. Kristen didn't want him to be unconscious, but needed him incapacitated as she took her revenge against the larger, stronger male. The vicious rage burning inside her demanded that John feel every blow she would rain down on his body as she used the same aluminum bat he had used so many times against her battered body.

John downed the first cup of coffee, and was working on a second when the effects of the drug began to work. He tried to stand and faltered, catching himself and bracing against the edge of the kitchen counter. Out of the corner of his eye, he saw her approach, bat in hand, and was barely able to raise his right arm to prevent the first blow from striking him square in his face. She could feel and hear the shattering of the bone as the bat struck just below his elbow, rendering his dominant arm useless. For a few brief seconds, Kristen froze, overwhelmed by nausea, and she feared she would not be able to continue, but the rage in John's eyes and the spite in his next words cleared her mind and further stoked her fury.

John glared at her. "You don't have the balls to kill me, bitch."

She answered his statement with a nasty blow to his right knee, dropping him immediately with a shattered kneecap. John struggled in his attempts to stand and she took one final swing, landing full force across his forehead with every ounce of pent up rage she had in her body. John's body flew backward into the lower cabinets with such force that the canisters on the counter scattered across the kitchen floor. The blow to his forehead sent shards of bone rushing toward his brain, and the impact of the back of his head against the cabinet crushed the rear of his skull. John's body slid down the front of the cabinet and fell to the kitchen floor with a dull thud.

Kristen stood over his body for several minutes, bat poised for another strike if needed, as she watched for any signs of life. John remained motionless and she bent down to check for a pulse. Finding none, she dropped to her knees as she stared at the broken and lifeless body of the man she once loved. That love had turned to hate after so many years of needless pain and abuse.

When the wave of nausea returned, she ran into the bathroom to purge her stomach of its contents, leaving her weak and covered in a cold sweat. With one final look at John's lifeless body, she climbed the stairs, showered, and dressed in traveling clothes. Her eyes kept wandering to the bedroom door where she expected John to rush her like a raging bull, but the house remained deadly silent as she picked up the bat and wiped the blood and bone fragments onto John's clothes and then carried the bat out to the Cadillac already loaded with her bags.

Kristen locked the doors, set the security alarm, and closed the garage door behind her as she backed the car out and slowly pulled away. She drove to a nearby softball complex and after wiping the bat down again, dropped the bat into a dugout to appear left behind in hopes that some team would pick it up, further confusing the police search for the murder weapon. She also dropped a small bag of trash into the dumpster at the edge of the park, its contents the container of hair coloring she had used the night before and a good eight inches of hair she had cut by herself. Her normally long dark hair was now a spiky blonde, totally changing her appearance, making her look a full ten years younger. She had carefully concealed the hair change underneath a stylish silk scarf wishing to eliminate any chance of a clerk or passerby recognizing the photos the police would soon be distributing.

Next she drove into the Miami airport and used curbside check in to obtain a boarding pass and check a bag for a flight to Amsterdam. She parked the car in a remote parking lot and took a shuttle to a car rental center just off the airport property. There she rented the car that would leave her stranded beside the interstate, still days away from her final destination.

As she walked, Kristen could see the lights of an upcoming exit glowing harshly in the night. The outline of a truck stop began to form as she walked closer and began to form a new plan. This time of night people would certainly not pick up a hitchhiker even one who appeared to be an attractive young female. She would have to figure out a way to continue her route west while concealing her identity as much as possible.

Kristen remained near the tree line where she could easily duck into the woods if detected as she approached the truck stop. She crept within fifty feet of the small eating establishment's parking lot and silently watched as travelers parked and went inside the building. Several businessmen made brief stops in the restaurant for a quick meal before returning to their vehicles to resume their trips. She considered trying to conceal herself in the rear of one of the many eighteen-wheeler trailers, but quickly talked herself out of that idea.

She watched with interest as a car with Texas plates pulled into the lot and a tall, dark-haired woman stepped from the vehicle. She first noticed the leather cowboy boots as they hit the pavement, followed by long legs covered in denim. Kristen watched the woman walk across the lot with grace and confidence until she disappeared inside the eatery.

She smiled as she realized that the woman had not locked the vehicle. With all the stealth she could muster, she ran across the lot and opened the driver's door. Just as she had hoped, the car, a Lincoln, had a button on the driver's side door that would open the trunk of the vehicle without a key. Her smile broadened as the trunk opened to reveal a large storage space. Kristen placed her duffle bag inside, and then placed her backpack near the side panel to use as a pillow to cushion her head during the bumpy ride. After locating the emergency pull inside the trunk, she climbed inside. The trunk closed securely and she waited for the driver to return, silently praying that the driver would be traveling west on her way back to Texas instead of heading further east, or worst yet south. She would have to gamble on her decision and prayed that Lady Luck would smile down upon her once more this day.

†

Carla Brooks had spent the majority of her adult life as a traveling salesperson for an agricultural firm located in Dallas, Texas. Her frequent travels across the south permitted her job to remain fresh and exciting to her, but it wreaked havoc on any attempt to have a social life or permanent relationship. Even though she had amassed a reasonable amount of savings, and owned a large ranch styled home on the outskirts of Austin, she was all alone in her life.

Tonight she had finished her scheduled route of stops for Florida and would be returning to Texas for the weekend. She had decided to visit the truck stop on a whim to dine on one of their greasy, but oh-so-tasty bacon cheeseburgers and fries. She ate her meal and then checked the time, deciding to drive a few more hours before finding a hotel for the night.

She paid her ticket, left a generous tip for the less-than-speedy service, and walked out into the night. A light mist had begun to fall and she hoped this would not be an omen of the night's weather. She opened her door, climbed behind the wheel, and headed back to the interstate with no idea of the stowaway tucked comfortably in her trunk.

Kristen could feel the acceleration of the vehicle as the driver merged onto the interstate and she could hear the soft hum of country music as it played on the radio. She pushed a button to illuminate the face of her watch and found that it was almost nine o'clock. Less than fourteen hours since she had started her plan rolling, and already it seemed an eternity ago. The trunk was warm, the tires hummed on the pavement, and soon she found her body being overtaken by sleep. Her exhausted mind and body dove deep into restful sleep as the car drove steadily west.

Carla drove for another two hours through a light rain before she decided to call it a night. She passed a sign advertising a national chain she frequented and took the following exit as instructed. She slipped from the car and went inside to register booking a king-sized room and a seven o'clock wake-up call for the next morning. Returning to her car, Carla pulled around to the back of the hotel away from the noise of the interstate.

Tired from the day's drive, she wanted nothing more than to retrieve her bag, take a long shower, and get a good night's rest. She turned the key in the trunk latch, and gasped when the trunk lid soared open and she looked down to find the young woman sleeping in her trunk.

"What the hell!"

Carla stared down at the young woman balled up in her trunk and noted the ugly yellowish bruises on her face. She stood transfixed, the rain falling more heavily now until the woman finally moved. Carla was relieved that at least the woman was alive and had not smothered to death or succumbed to carbon monoxide poisoning.

Kristen heard the woman's shout and her eyes flew open in full panic mode to find the woman staring down at her. Her intent had been to use the emergency release to exit the trunk when the woman left the car to check in to her hotel, but instead, her body collapsed in exhaustion and she had not realized they had stopped until the trunk flew open.

Kristen instinctively reached behind her for the nine millimeter and then thought better of the move. Meaning no harm to anyone, she would use the handgun only as a means of protection if endangered. The lady looking down in shock into her trunk did not appear to intend to harm her, even though, with her formidable size, she probably could. Kristen eased her hand away and stared back at the woman.

She watched the shock fade away from the woman's face before a smile replaced it. "Well, this has certainly got to be a story worth telling," she said. The woman reached a hand into the trunk, offering Kristen assistance while she struggled to sit upright. "But why don't we hear it inside out of this rain?"

Kristen sent her a warm smile hoping that the woman would accept the story she had carefully crafted.

"Let's grab our bags and make a dash of it," the woman said.

Kristen, feeling the stiffness in her body, grimaced as she took the offered hand and crawled gingerly from the trunk.

The woman handed the two unfamiliar bags to her before grabbing the large bag from the trunk. She stepped quickly over to the covered sidewalk leaving Kristen standing in the pouring rain.

Out of the rain the woman turned and looked at her.

Kristen had two options, take off running with her bags, or accept the generous offer of at least temporary shelter from a lovely stranger. The cold rain was soaking into her bones, making her decision an easy one. She ran quickly to the cover and followed the woman to a large business-class room.

Carla placed her bag down beside the king-sized bed and turned to look at the young woman who stood dripping in the doorway of her hotel room. "Close the door and put your bags over there." She pointed to a small table next to the television and then walked into the bathroom to grab a couple of towels. "Here, catch." She tossed a thick towel to the young woman and began wiping the rain from her face and arms.

"Thanks." The stranger caught the towel and began drying off as well while watching her cautiously.

Satisfied that she was as dry as she was going to get for the time being, Carla sat down on the end of the bed. "My name is Carla."

Kristen had also finished drying off and, when Carla spoke, she sat down on the edge of the recliner approximately ten feet away from the bed. "My name is Kristen."

"Care to tell me how and why you came to be sleeping in the trunk of my car?"

"I left my husband today. I rented a car that broke down on me on the interstate and I had no other choice but to continue walking for the night. I saw the lights of the truck stop looming ahead so I headed there. I was hiding when I saw you pull into the parking lot with Texas tags. I noticed that you failed to lock your doors, and an idea popped into my head." She paused to take a breath. "I thought I could steal away in your trunk and then when you stopped for the night, I could slip out of the trunk while you were inside checking in. I didn't take into account how tired I was and how the warmth of the trunk and the hum of the tires would lull me to sleep."

Carla listened with a slight grin of amusement as Kristen continued her tale. "I have to admit it was a very clever plan, but you do realize the possibility you faced of dying from carbon monoxide poisoning?"

"It would have been an easier death than to admit defeat and allow my husband to enjoy my failure as he drove me home, threatening and delivering a beating I would remember for a long time for my disobedience."

That statement quickly removed the grin from Carla's face. "So that's where the bruises came from?"

"Yes, I have survived beatings regularly from him for several years, and I finally realized if I didn't flee soon, I would die by his hands."

"I know this will probably sound condescending, but did you ever make a report to the authorities?"

"Well, that was a huge part of the problem. My husband's brother was the Sheriff, and anytime I made a report, the charges would disappear. He was even able to cover up the numerous hospital visits with tales of substance abuse. He threatened to put me away in a mental hospital if I continued to try to expose his brother."

Carla's first instinct was to wrap her arms around the woman and give her a long, comforting hug, but she allowed Kristen to maintain a comfortable distance. "So what's your plan from here?"

"I need to make it to Mexico. I don't want to tell you any details, because I don't want to endanger you or anyone else."

"Do you really think your husband's control would place me in danger?"

"When his brother learns of my escape he will come after me with a vengeance. I have set up several smoke screens that should give me a bit of a lead before they find out I haven't left the country. The rental car failure threw me a twist I hadn't planned. I've modified my appearance a bit, but the longer I remain in the States the more likely my chances of detection are." Kristen shivered as if a sudden chill blew over her.

"Why don't you shower and change into something warm?" Carla noticed what she thought were chills shaking

Kristen's body again. "When was the last time you ate something?"

"Last night at supper," she answered.

"Well, pizza is about the only thing we can get delivered. Pick your poison and I'll order it while you warm up."

"I love everything on it except anchovies." Kristen stood and reached into her pocket to pull out a twenty.

"Keep it, this one is on me." Carla walked over to the phone and looked up the number of a pizza delivery service. She ordered a large, thick-crust pizza with the works, a two-liter bottle of coke, and then sat back to wait for the delivery. She could hear the shower start in the bathroom and knew that she could not refuse to help the young lady in her flight.

She had laid her head down on the back of the recliner and had drifted off to sleep when she felt the slight touch of a warm hand on her arm.

"Your turn," Kristen whispered softly.

Carla jumped slightly at the touch, startled by how easily she had drifted off. It was getting late and a nice hot shower would feel good. She shuffled through her bag until she found a pair of shorts and a T-shirt. She pointed to a pile of cash sitting by the door. "There's the money for the pizza, when it arrives. Don't wait on me if it gets here before I finish showering. Eat while it is still hot."

Kristen nodded and Carla walked into the bathroom. She was lost in the comfort of the shower when the pizza was delivered, and when she dried off and dressed, she was disappointed to find an empty room when she returned. She just assumed Kristen had taken off when she slipped into the shower. What she failed to realize was that her bags were still sitting on the table where she had placed them.

The click of the key in the door caught her attention and a few seconds later, Kristen walked through the door carrying a bucket of ice.

"Sorry if I startled you. The soda was hot so I went in search of some ice." She poured them both a drink and sat near the end of the couch so Carla could join her in devouring the pizza.

"This is really good," Kristen said between bites of her fourth slice of pizza.

Carla just smiled and watched as she finished off another two slices before reaching her fill of the heavily topped pizza.

Carla refilled their cups with soda and sat back on the couch. "I'm on my way home to Austin and I wouldn't mind some company for the ride if you want to stay with me. There is one condition though."

"What's that?"

"You have to ride up front and not in my damned trunk." She chuckled.

"You have a deal." For the first time that evening, Carla saw a warm and brilliant smile fill Kristen's face.

"I have a wake-up call at seven and it is getting late."

"I saw some extra pillows and a blanket in the closet." Kristen stood to retrieve the linens.

Carla thought about offering a portion of the king-sized bed to her, but again thought it wise to allow Kristen to maintain her space. She helped her create a sleeping area on the couch and then turned the lights out and crept into the bed. The cool sheets and pillow top mattress had to be much more comfortable than the couch, and she fell asleep in minutes after she snuggled under the covers.

A few hours later, she felt a weight on the edge of the bed and then felt the warmth of Kristen's body as she snuggled into her back in silence. Comforted by the warmth and closeness of her guest, Carla closed her eyes, smiled, and slipped back into sleep.

†

When she awoke the next morning, she found herself cuddled into Kristen, her arm protectively wrapped around her waist. Carla was surprised to find Kristen had joined her in the bed as she slept. When she realized her arm was draped around Kristen, Carla moved it immediately.

Kristen smiled warmly. "Good morning."

"Good morning. Have you been awake long?"

"No, not long at all. The couch wasn't very comfortable though, so I climbed into bed with you. I hope you don't mind."

"No, not at all. I just hope I didn't kick you or snore in your ear."

Kristen chuckled. "I just rubbed your side and you quit snoring."

Carla blushed and started to sit up.

Kristen pushed her back down. "Why don't you lay still while I go get us some coffee?"

Carla watched as she left the bed and went to the bathroom.

In the bathroom Kristen recalled the blush on Carla's face. *Did the thought of my hands on her body embarrass her?* Kristen brushed her tangled hair, and then slipped on a pair of tennis shoes. "How do you like your coffee, Carla?"

"Hot, strong, and black."

"I'll be back in just a few." Kristen slipped out the door.

As promised, she delivered several hot cups of coffee to the room and she and Carla shared them as they prepared for the day's travel.

"I am hoping we can make it at least to the Texas border by tonight." Carla sat on the couch and sipped her coffee.

"That would be fantastic." For a moment, Kristen had forgotten her plight, and Carla's comment, served to remind her she was in fact a wanted fugitive, or at least would be in just a few days.

†

After drinking the last cup of coffee, Carla took a shower, dressed in jeans, a pullover, and cowboy boots. She finished packing her bag and took it out to the trunk while Kristen showered and dressed. As she walked to the door with her bag, she couldn't help but notice the butt of the pistol concealed between several items of clothing in Kristen's bag. Normally the sight would have unsettled her a bit, but given Kristen's story she wasn't at all surprised or uneasy that her traveling companion was armed. She was a much smaller woman than Carla was, and would need every ounce of protection she could get to survive in this world.

Carla was out in the car fiddling around in the back seat, placing her briefcase and store samples in safe storage. Normally, these items would be within arm's reach of her in the front seat. She smiled. She now had someone to talk with riding beside her.

Kristen walked out dressed neatly in jeans, a dark pullover, and leather boots. They were comfortable traveling clothes and they looked very natural on her as well. Kristen placed her bags in the trunk and dropped her leather jacket on the back seat.

"All set?"

"Most definitely." Kristen gave another one of her beautiful smiles.

"Are you hungry?"

"Not really."

"Why don't we drive for a bit and then we can stop for some breakfast when one of us gets hungry."

"That sounds good to me. But I get to treat this morning, Carla."

"You won't get an argument from me." She drove to the front office to drop off her keys and pick up her receipt.

They pulled out onto Interstate 10 into a glorious, sunny morning that held a promise of clear skies all day. They rode in silence for a while until Carla decided it was time to learn a little more about her quiet passenger.

"So, tell me a bit about you."

"There's really not much to tell. I'm thirty-four and have lived in South Florida almost all my life. I was married to John for five years and was a stay-at-home wife to him."

"No children?" Carla immediately regretted asking when she saw the look on Kristen's face.

The anguish written across her face told Carla more than she cared to know of the pain and suffering this young woman had endured.

"I was pregnant once. But after the sonogram revealed the baby was a little girl, John beat me until I miscarried and threatened to kill me if I allowed myself to get pregnant again."

"Sounds like a real bastard."

"In the beginning he was the sweetest, most caring man a woman could ask for, but that all changed when he started doing coke a few years ago. When the beatings first started, I blamed myself, thinking I had done something to provoke him. When they continued, I realized it wasn't my fault at all."

"Men like that need to be shot."

Kristen remained quiet after her comment.

Carla noticed that the mood in the car had gone quite somber. A sign for a roadside breakfast place came up. "Are you hungry yet?"

"I think I could eat." Kristen gave a slight grin, which was a welcome sight for Carla.

"Well, let's see how this place works out." She exited and turned into the diner.

The food was quite good and they both ate their fill before resuming their route west. The day had blossomed beautifully and they could smell the distant salt in the air as their travels brought them closer to Gulf waters.

"Have you ever been to Mexico?" Carla asked.

"Just a quick trip to Mexico City for a short honeymoon."

"It is a wild and beautiful country filled with wide open spaces and humble people."

"Do you travel there often?"

"Not often, but I want to spend more time investigating retirement prospects down there someday. The value of the American dollar is quite strong in Mexico, and if you live wisely, you can live like a queen for a quarter of the money you would spend here in the States. But you must really like beans," Carla teased.

"I love Mexican food so hopefully I will be at home with all the beans and rice," Kristen shot back.

"Do you have any idea where you are heading?" Carla asked.

"I have a small villa in the mountains picked out and hopefully no one has purchased it in the last week."

"That sounds very lovely."

"I hope to try my hand at painting once I get settled in. I have always enjoyed drawing and the landscape holds a lot of promise for beautiful pictures. Maybe I can set up a little roadside stand and sell paintings to the gringos who come as tourists." She laughed.

The sound of her laughter brought a smile to Carla's face. It was a heartwarming sound. She doubted Kristen often had an opportunity to laugh.

The morning passed quickly as they made small talk and commented on the passing landscape. The car had become very quiet and when Carla looked across the seat, she found that Kristen had curled up in the seat and was quietly napping. *Such a beautiful soul*, she thought as she watched her sleeping form. How could anyone be so cruel to another human being?

The sun began the late afternoon decline as she drove for another hour before the gas gauge notified her it was time to stop and refuel. She carefully maneuvered the car off the interstate into a gas station and closed the door quietly behind her when she departed the car, hoping to not wake Kristen as she slept. She fueled the car and paid for the purchase before slipping behind the steering wheel once again.

Kristen stretched in the seat, slowly waking. "Would you mind if I took a bathroom break while we are stopped?"

"Go right ahead." She pulled the car up to the outdoor restrooms. "Would you care for anything from inside?"

"A bottle of water would be great." Her smile melted Carla's heart.

Carla poured a strong cup of coffee for herself and paid for her purchases. When she returned to the car, Kristen was standing beside it looking down the interstate. "Do you need to stretch your legs a bit?"

"No, I am fine, but thanks for asking. Where are we?"

"Just about two hundred miles from the Texas state line."

"I hadn't realized I had slept for that long." Kristen took the bottle of water Carla handed her.

"You had a nice nap," Carla said with a warm smile.

Carla watched her flinch as a local Sheriff's Department cruiser drove by. Carla caught her eye and nodded back to the car. Kristen gladly sat back in the car and unconsciously slumped deeper into the seat. Her distress was very apparent to Carla who issued up a silent prayer that her passenger would make her escape successfully and be able to live her life without future threats of horrible beatings from the person she had loved.

Carla pulled back onto the interstate and asked, "How about a thick, juicy steak tonight?"

"That sounds wonderful. Do you know a good spot?"

"As a matter of fact, yes I do. It should be about another two hours ahead and close to a hotel for the night as well."

Kristen smiled and Carla said, "It's a done deal then."

"I can drive for a while if you get tired."

"Thanks, I am good for a while yet."

"Do you ever get tired of all the traveling?"

"Sometimes. Then I think of myself cooped up inside an office all day and I figure the travel isn't so bad after all."

"Never been married?"

"Lord no. With all this travel who would want to be stuck with me?"

"I think someone would be very lucky to be stuck with you." Her reply caused Carla to blush profusely. "I am sorry if I embarrassed you by being nosy."

"That was just a very sweet thing for you to say."

"So never anyone special?"

All right if she wants to play this game, I will play it. Carla thought about her answer. "A few years ago there was a very special person in my life."

"What happened?"

"She decided she needed someone to hold onto every night instead of just three nights over the weekend." A note of sadness crept into her voice no matter how hard she tried to hide it.

Kristen reached across the seat and placed her hand on Carla's shoulder. "I am sorry for prying into your business."

Carla's shoulder tingled under her touch and she blushed again at the feel of the woman's hand. It had been a long time since she was close to another woman as her body was now reminding her.

"You weren't prying, Kristen. I could have chosen to answer differently, but I don't feel a need to hide my feelings from you for some reason."

They went silent after that and they drove in silence until the exit to the steak house came into sight. "Ah, here we are." She guided the car through the exit and into the parking lot.

""They do make one of the best I have found. I have eaten at steak houses all over the South, but none as consistently good as this one."

Kristen ate every bite of her steak and finished off her baked potato as well. "You were right, Carla. The steaks are to die for. I don't know if I have ever had a better meal."

She moved to reached for the bill. "This is my treat, you got breakfast remember?"

Kristen smiled warmly and nodded.

"I don't know about you, but I think I have traveled enough for one day."

"I slept most of the day and I am still tired, so I can imagine how tired you are."

"There is a nice clean hotel just a little farther down this road."

"Sounds good to me."

"Should I get one bed or two?"

Kristen smiled sheepishly. "Would you mind sharing again? I really enjoyed having you next to me."

"Not at all. You seem to be able to deal with my snoring." Carla chuckled. "One it is, then."

†

Carla pulled into the driveway and went inside to check in. She returned minutes later and pulled the car around the back of the hotel. They climbed from the car and took their bags into the room.

"Would you like to shower first?" Carla asked.

"No, you go ahead and I will wait."

"I will be done in a hurry then."

"Enjoy yourself."

Carla slipped into the bathroom for a hot, relaxing shower and when she finished, she knew she would sleep well that night. She brushed her teeth and dressed in her pajamas before leaving the bathroom. "Your turn."

"I'll be done in a few."

Carla locked the door to the room and turned all of the lights off except the one next to the side of the bed Kristen would be sleeping on. She crept between the sheets, laid her head on the pillow, and closed her eyes.

Several minutes later, Carla felt the bed move as Kristen climbed in. She kept her eyes closed as she breathed in the clean scent of Kristen so near her. She felt her body tremble with desire as she pressed her body close.

"Are you cold?"

"No." Carla was barely able to breathe.

Carla felt Kristen move, and then felt the brush of soft lips searching for hers in a tender kiss. The trembling intensified as Kristen's tongue swirled past her lips and entered her mouth. She willed her body to stop trembling, but when their tongues made contact, Carla knew she no longer had control of her body.

Kristen's hand worked its way beneath Carla's top and caressed her skin with soft strokes. She was amazed by the way her body reacted to her touch as she kissed her deeply. Carla's arm encircled her body to pull Kristen closer and when her hand made contact with her naked body, she groaned loudly. She had intended to seduce her when she entered the bed and Carla fell so easily to her charms. She pulled her closer and when Kristen's hand covered her right breast, she heard Carla moan from the sheer sensuality of her touch.

Kristen had never been with another woman before, but she sensed exactly what to do to make love to Carla. She broke the kiss long enough to look deep into Carla's eyes. "I want to feel your skin on mine." Her hand raised the hem of Carla's top.

Carla lifted up to remove the top and then looked back at a smiling Kristen. "All of it." She sat up on the bed to pull Carla's pajama bottoms off and tossed them from the bed.

The pleading look in her eyes made Kristen smile and her instincts took over. She moved on top of Carla and slowly lowered her body. The warmth and softness of Carla's body enveloped her as she melted into her. She could feel the heat and moistness between Carla's thighs as it made contact with her skin. Kristen could feel her own dampness growing as her arousal grew rampantly.

She nuzzled into her neck as Carla's hands began to caress her back, the vibration of her soft moans increasing as Carla's body began to move beneath her, her hips rolling up to press their bodies together.

"You feel so good," she breathed against Carla's neck. "Oh, Kristen, you have me so turned on."

She moved further up Carla's body until their mounds met and she lowered her lips toward Carla's. "I want to make you feel so good." She gasped as their aroused clits made contact. "Oh my God, that feels heavenly."

Kristen's tongue traced along her lips as Carla's hand slid down to her hips, pulling Kristen's body into hers as the passion between them ignited further. Kristen began to tremble as their tongues touched, swirling together deep inside her mouth. With the encouragement of Carla's hand, she found her hips grinding into her body, sending a delightful flow of pleasure through her. She convulsed into Carla as she felt the first orgasm she had experienced in years.

"Oh my God," she cried out as she exploded with intense pleasure.

Carla wrapped her arms around her and held her tight as she continued to quake with aftershocks of pleasure.

Kristen lifted her head to look into Carla's face, enchanted by the look of desire she found pooling in her eyes. Without a word spoken between them, she moved lower on Carla's body until her mouth made contact with Carla's soft breast.

Her tongue softly licked across the firm nipple and she felt it grow hard beneath her soft strokes. Her right hand fondled Carla's left breast, her fingertips teasing the sensitive nipple as her lips wrapped around the other.

"Yes, Kristen." Carla's hand stroked through her hair still damp from the shower.

She opened her mouth and filled it with the flesh of Carla's breast as she sucked her like a child. Her body was overflowing with desire as her hand slipped between them and she felt the silky wetness of another woman's body. Her groans reverberated against Carla's skin as her fingers parted her lower lips and her fingers sank into the velvety warmth.

When Carla felt Kristen's soft fingers glide into her she felt she would go insane with the intense pleasure each movement brought to her. She felt Kristen's teeth graze across her nipple and her mind exploded with beautiful lights as her orgasm surged through her.

Kristen could feel Carla's muscles grasping at her fingers as her body released and a flood of juices filled her palm. "Oh yes, baby," she cried out as she gasped to find her next breath.

Kristen slowly withdrew her fingers and lifted them to her lips. She was eager to taste Carla and her tongue welcomed the taste that coated her fingers. "You taste so good." She moved farther down Carla's body until she rested between her trembling thighs.

Her fingers shook with excitement as they gently parted her lips and her tongue gently probed her wetness, lapping at her sweetness as Carla writhed on the bed. The taste overwhelmed Kristen and her tongue went wild inside her as she drank greedily. Carla's hand held her head in place as she ground her hips onto the tongue thrusting in and out of her.

Her tongue rolled across Carla's blood gorged clit, causing her to groan loudly. She replaced her tongue with two fingers as her lips closed around her clit, her fingers reaching deep inside, as her tongue swirled furiously around her clit.

Carla arched her back as her orgasm surged through her and she released a flood of juice onto Kristen's face.

Kristen climbed back up her body and molded into her as she felt the tremors run through her. Carla's arms encircled her and held her close as she slowly gained control.

She listened to the wild beating of Carla's heart until it began to slow back to normal and then looked up into her face.

Carla smiled at her and then rolled her onto her back. Her lips covered Kristen's and she tasted herself on her lover's face. Her hand gently caressed her soft breasts, feeling her nipples grow hard beneath her touch as their tongues danced together. She covered Carla's hand with her own as she guided it down her body until it rested on top of her steaming mound.

Carla's mouth covered her breast as her fingers entered Kristen, reaching deep inside her as her fingers curled and caressed her interior walls. Kristen's hips thrashed wildly on the bed as Carla's fingers plunged in and out, and her mind soared with pleasure.

"Faster, baby," Kristen cried as her nails raked down Carla's back.

Carla thrust her fingers faster and deeper into her until she felt Kristen's muscles begin to contract around them. Her teeth nibbled the tip of her nipple and she cried out with pleasure.

"Oh, dear God, yes, Carla, I'm coming," Kristen cried, her body bucked wildly on the bed.

Carla could feel the rush of moisture fill her hand and she slowly removed her fingers. She moved down the bed and buried her face in Kristen's wetness as she exploded in a second orgasm. Her thighs clamped tightly onto Carla's head as her tongue drove deep inside her.

When she relaxed, Kristen reached down and pulled Carla back on top of her. She kissed her passionately as a third climax gripped her, and she locked her heels behind

Carla's grinding hips. She thrust into her body until she exhausted the pent up passion in her and she collapsed onto her, her body trembling with release.

Carla barely had the strength left to roll over onto her back as she lay panting, trying to catch her breath. Kristen rolled onto her side facing Carla and looked into her face. "Thank you," she whispered as she laid her head on her shoulder.

"Why are you thanking me?"

"For allowing me to feel wanted, even if it was for just a short time." She smiled as her tears ran down her cheeks.

"Kristen, you are a beautiful woman and don't let anyone ever tell you different. You got a raw deal in life so far, so you are due for a change of luck."

Kristen looked up to her with tears in her eyes. "I haven't exactly been truthful with you."

"What do you mean?" Carla stroked her hair.

"I did leave my husband, but I didn't leave him alive. I drugged his coffee and then I used the same bat he used on me so many times to crush his skull in." She broke down in tears, sobbing uncontrollably on Carla's shoulder.

"So you gave him what he deserved. I had already gathered there was more to your story."

Kristen looked at her in shock. "You understand I am telling you that I am a murderer, don't you?"

"No, you are telling me you did what you had to do to protect yourself." Carla lifted her chin.

"You could be in so much trouble if we, if I get caught."

"We are not going to get caught and even if we do, I can just claim that I was just helping you out by giving you a ride."

"I can't afford to put you in any more jeopardy. Tomorrow I will find a bus to take me across the border to Mexico."

"You will do no such thing! Don't you think they will be keeping an eye on all bus traffic?"

"That's a risk I will have to take."

"No, it's not. I have a ton of vacation that I need to take, so I am going to take a day or two to see you settled in Mexico."

"Carla, you can't."

"Yes, I can and I will. We will stop by my place to allow me to pick up a few things and we will head for the border. If all goes well, we will be across the border before they find him."

"Carla…" Kristen started, but Carla placed a finger on her lips.

"Rest now and we will deal with tomorrow, tomorrow." She kissed the top of Kristen's head.

"Thank you." She snuggled into Carla and drifted off to sleep.

Carla held her until her own weariness took over and her hand slipped off her shoulder to rest on her hip.

†

The next morning, Carla woke up to the sound of the shower running. She walked into the bathroom and peeked behind the shower curtain. "Would you mind some company?"

"Not at all." Kristen held her hand out to her.

Carla stepped into the back of the shower and looked at her, the water flowing down the front of her body. At that moment, she doubted she had ever seen anyone so beautiful.

Kristen stepped from the flow of the water and they kissed, softly at first and then passionately as their hands explored one another's body. She pressed Carla against the shower wall as her fingers penetrated her. "Come with me, Carla," she said between kisses as she guided Carla's hand down.

They came together, their bodies shaking with bliss as they clutched one another. They finished bathing and dried their bodies before returning to the bedroom to dress. Carla was sitting on the edge of the bed pulling on her boots when Kristen pushed her back onto the bed and straddled her hips.

"I am going to have a hard time letting you go." She leaned down to kiss Carla.

"We have a few more days yet." Carla pulled her down for a deep kiss.

"If you don't stop kissing me like that, we will not make it out of this room today," she teased.

"Do I need to remind you that you started this?" Carla's hands ran down her sides.

"No, not at all." Kristen grinned as she stepped back off the bed. "We had better get moving." She pulled Carla up from the bed.

Carla went to the office to check out while Kristen loaded their bags. She walked back carrying two cups of coffee and handed one to her. "We can stop for breakfast later if you get hungry."

"What I am hungry for is not on any menu." She smiled at Carla.

Carla blushed as she closed the door behind her and walked around to the driver's side and sat behind the wheel. She placed her coffee in the cup holder and turned to Kristen, desire glowing in her eyes. "You have awakened a powerful hunger in me, too."

"How long before we reach your place?"

"Another six hours if we drive straight through."

"Let's drive straight through." She laid her head on Carla's shoulder and rested her hand on her thigh.

Carla pulled the car out onto the interstate and they stopped only once to refill the car with gas and to take a break to stretch their legs.

†

The sun was dipping near the horizon when Carla slowed the car and turned off a main road onto a narrow lane. Kristen watched as a beautiful ranch style home came into view and Carla pulled into an enclosed garage.

"Welcome to my home," Carla said when she turned the engine off.

"This place is beautiful."

They left the garage and walked through a large kitchen into an even larger family room. Kristen looked out the sliding glass door, saw a large enclosed swimming pool, and smiled back at Carla.

Carla took her hand and walked her through the house until they reached the large master bedroom. A teakwood bed was the centerpiece of the room and Kristen turned in Carla's arms. She lifted the shirt over her head, working on the fasteners of Carla's jeans as their lips met. She kissed her softly and then her lips kissed down her chest as she removed her bra.

Her mouth covered a breast as her hands opened Carla's jeans and she reached around to cup her ass. Her moans filled the room as she turned her back to the bed and lowered her to a sitting position. She pulled off Carla's boots and socks and then removed her jeans. She pushed her back and knelt at the edge of the bed. She lifted Carla's thighs and draped them over her shoulders as her tongue traced the

191

outline of her lips through the silky panties. She slid a finger inside the crotch of the panties and stroked through Carla's dampness.

"I must have some of this." She kissed the inside of Carla's thigh.

Kristen removed the panties and used her tongue to part Carla's lips, stroking the length of them with a soft tongue. "This is what I hunger for," she said as her tongue entered Carla, lapping up the growing wetness.

"I am hungry, too," Carla said.

Kristen quickly stripped out of her clothes and climbed onto the bed as she straddled her head with her hips. She returned her face between Carla's thighs and continued her sensual kiss as Carla's hands guided Kristen's hips down to her face. Carla parted her lips with her fingertip as her tongue brushed lightly over the sensitive flesh glistening with moisture.

Carla could feel Kristen's erect nipples drag across her skin as her head moved between her thighs and her body burned with passion. They kissed one another into intense orgasms and then lay panting on the bed.

"How about a swim to cool us off and then I will fix us a light meal?"

"I've been dying to try the pool since we arrived." Kristen took her hand and they walked out to the pool. They dove into the deep end and swam to the shallow end together.

"I never knew water could feel so good against my skin," she said.

Carla sat next to her on the pool steps. "Remarkable isn't it? How different it feels when you are totally bare."

"We had a pool, but hardly ever used it."

"I swim every weekend. It is great exercise."

"You are in very good shape." Kristen trailed a fingertip down Carla's arm. "Follow me." She stood and stepped from the pool.

Kristen had spotted a bottle of baby oil and a thick towel sitting on a lounge chair. She stopped to pick them up and took her hand to lead her to the diving board. She spread the towel down the length of the board and then laid her down on her back.

She straddled the diving board and draped Carla's thighs over her own as she moved as close as she could to her. With a look of pure devilment in her eyes, she popped the lid on the baby oil, dribbled a line of oil down Carla's right arm, and then tucked the bottle between their bodies as she coated the arm with the silky oil and then repeated the process with her left arm.

She lifted Carla's left leg and rested it on her shoulder as she covered it with oil as her lips kissed a burning trail from her knee down the inside of Carla's thigh. When both her legs were coated with oil she moved close to Carla's body again. "Lock your legs around my back."

Carla locked her heels together behind Kristen's back and watched with great anticipation as Kristen poured a palm full of the oil in her hand. Instead of leaning down and rubbing the oil into her skin, Carla watched as she rubbed her palms together and then she began caressing the oil onto her breasts. Carla felt her nipples grow hard as she watched her hands coat her breasts and nipples.

Kristen saw her tongue lick across her lower lip as she watched her hands move over her body. She took the bottle and dribbled a flow of oil down between her breasts. Her eyes watched the oil flow down the front of Kristen's body until it reached the crest of her mound. Her hands caressed her body until her front coated with oil, as her eyes locked with Carla's. "Your turn," she whispered as she lifted the bottle and filled Carla's navel with the oil.

She smiled and leaned forward to grasp the end of the diving board with her hands as she lowered her trunk onto Carla's and used her body to massage the oil into her skin. Their bodies moved fluidly together in the silky oil as Kristen's mouth covered Carla's with a fevered kiss.

Carla used her hands to pull Kristen onto her, and when their hips rubbed together, it sent waves of pleasure through them. She slowly ground her hips into Carla as their arousal intensified, leaving them breathless and shaking in one another's arms.

Kristen led them into the shower and bathed the oil from their bodies. She wrapped them in thick, warm robes after the shower and held Carla in her arms. "Why couldn't I have met you five years ago?"

"At least we had the opportunity to meet now." Carla smoothed Kristen's hair with her hand.

"Too late, my life is now ruined."

"No, my dear, when you step across the border tomorrow, your life has just begun."

"If only it were that simple."

"Why can't it be? A new life, a new identity, and if you are careful, you will never be caught."

"Will I find another who treats me as lovingly as you?"

"If you wish for her hard enough, she will come."

"I will keep that in mind." Kristen dried her tears.

"Are you ready for some food?"

"That's right, you did promise to feed me."

Carla sat her at the kitchen table and then prepared a meal of fruits, cheeses, and wine. They shared the meal and then sat up in the bed talking deep into the night.

†

The next morning after a long shower together, Carla pulled out a small bag and started to pack for their trip.

"I have to go on alone from the border. I will not involve you any further in my madness."

"I will see you to your destination as promised."

"No, if you do that, then you will know where I am. If they ever track me to you, you will have to lie and I won't have that. All they need to know is you gave a ride to a stranger."

"His family scares you that much?"

"Yes, they do. I would die if anything happened to you because of me."

"Nothing will happen to me."

"That's because it has to be this way. I can't thank you for all you have given me and been to me."

"There is no need for thanks. I have greatly enjoyed our time together."

The final ride south was difficult for them both. Carla knew she was letting a good woman slip through her hands and Kristen knew that life without Carla was going to be miserable.

At the border, Carla was asked for her identification and she told Kristen to wrap up in a blanket and pretend she was asleep. The guard who checked them through bought Carla's story that Kristen was her younger sister.

"She has been sick all day with morning sickness, so please don't wake her."

He smiled at her. "My wife is going through the same thing. What is your business in Mexico?"

"This is her first child and we are traveling to purchase a hand-made crib."

"Matamoras has many merchants who craft furniture, so you should find many good deals."

"That is exactly where we are heading."

"Have a good day, miss." He waved them through.

"What are you going to tell them on the way back through, when you have no pregnant sister or baby crib?"

"I will have an order for a crib, but hopefully they won't remember you were traveling with me."

"What will you do with a baby crib?"

"I will call and cancel the order when I return home, or maybe keep it for a future baby shower."

"You are so clever."

†

It was a short drive to Matamoras. They were getting close to their destination and Carla slowed the car, wanting to prolong the moment when she would say goodbye, and Kristen knew it.

With a deep sigh, she pulled up in front of the bus station. "There is a small restaurant just two blocks down from here. I will wait there for three hours in case you change your mind. It will be dark then and easier to cross back into the States."

Carla parked the car and walked to the trunk to get her bags while she went in to purchase her ticket. When Kristen returned, Carla could see the tears in her eyes. She took her in her arms and hugged her close. Carla then kissed her passionately for the last time. "Three hours." She climbed back into the car and drove away, tears blurring her vision.

†

Kristen picked up her bags and walked into the bus station after watching Carla drive away. She found a seat in the rear of the station close to the bus she would soon be taking as she continued her adventure. Kristen painfully watched the minutes tick by on the large station clock. She longed to tuck herself safely away in Carla's arms, but she knew neither of them would be safe in the States if she stayed. When the call to board the bus finally came, she looked at the clock one last time. Twenty minutes and Carla would drive away. Her heart broke as she climbed the steps to the bus and rode away from the city and the first person who had truly loved her.

†

Carla parked her car and went inside the restaurant where she ordered a bottle of water and chips with salsa. She had no appetite, but she picked at the chips to help pass the time. She didn't know what she would do if Kristen walked through the door, but they would come up with some plan to be together. It had to be her choice though. Carla would not make that decision for her even though she desperately wanted to be with her.

At three hours and five minutes, Carla pulled back into the bus station. She went inside in search of Kristen and, had she still been there, she planned to insist she return home with her. She would find a good attorney for her and together they would fight for her freedom. Kristen was nowhere in sight and, sadly, Carla returned to her car to make the long drive home alone.

The house felt so empty without the sounds of Kristen's laughter or her voice as she called out Carla's name. Carla returned to the road quickly to occupy her thoughts as she tried to move past the longing that made her body ache.

Kristen stepped off the bus after the long ride and walked directly to the realtor's office. She rode with her out to the villa she wanted to purchase. She was very pleased by what she saw and when they returned to town, she made the purchase much more cheaply than she had anticipated. She also purchased a small car and, after purchasing some basics for her new home, she drove back into the mountains.

†

Two months gave way to three. No matter how hard she tried, Carla could not erase the memory of Kristen from her mind or her body. Then one night, when she returned home from an exceptionally long trip, she sat at her dining room table thumbing through a large stack of mail when a letter fell from the stack into her lap.

The handwriting on the envelope looked unfamiliar to her as she eagerly opened the seal. Inside was a one-page note, which read:

My Dearest Carla,
I hope this note finds life treating you well. I have settled into my new home and have begun painting the beautiful landscapes of this wondrous country, but my heart still longs for you.
Your words on our last night together still ring in my ears. You said, "Wish for her hard enough and she will come." Carla, my love, I am wishing for you the hardest I can. Will you join me? My freedom means nothing to me if I must live without you.

Please join me when you can. I have enclosed my address and pray you return to me soon.
I love you.
K

Carla picked up the envelope and looked at the postmark. It was dated nearly three weeks ago.

Carla's heart raced with excitement as she ran to her bedroom and packed a small bag. She tossed it into the back seat and pulled out of her driveway, heading south to the woman she loved.

A Taste of Heaven

You lie naked on top of crumpled sheets unable to sleep. Sweat beads on your skin, not only from the sweltering heat outside, but also from the desire burning within you. I lie stretched across the bed, listening to the sound of your breathing, and the breakers that are licking against the shore. The window is open, but the air is deathly still. I open my eyes and see your face, aglow with bliss, your eyes tightly closed to delay the inevitable end to your pleasure.

I watch as a bead of sweat trickles down between your breasts and slowly runs down your side. My tongue, tempted, moves down to catch the bead and lick upward along the salty trail. You vibrate from your moans as my tongue gently bathes your skin, swirling and caressing to the sweet valley between your breasts. My hand floats across the softness of your belly, following the contours of your body as the spasms begin to fade and you reach out for my hand, taking it gently in yours. Tonight you have tasted love, and hunger for more.

Our hands move slowly down the front of your body as my lips tug gently at your growing nipple and we reach wetness together. Our fingers touch, then entwine, joining together as one as we explore the treasure hidden between your thighs, moving slowly together in the silky delight as your body awakens to the need burning deep within you. You open your thighs allowing our fingers passage into the source of your fire as my mouth leaves your breast to kiss up your neck to your lips. Our tongues meet, teasing, and swirling around one another as our fingers glide in and out of you, your hips thrusting upward on top of the soaked sheets. Our kiss muffles the whimpering of your voice as your climax looms near.

I break the kiss and look into your eyes as the passion so deeply concealed before awakens, and your eyes sparkle with love and the joy of our lovemaking as you release a flood of pleasure so intense it takes my breath away. Your breath whispers my name as your muscles pulse around our fingers resting deep within you.

We withdraw slowly, each movement causing a new spasm to vibrate inside you, and I raise your hand to my lips. My tongue flicks out to capture the velvety smooth juice coating your fingers and I moan as the taste assaults my senses. You watch, eyes wide, as each finger disappears between my lips as I cleanse them of their sweet offering.

Our eyes lock and I smile as I kiss the tips of your fingers and then place your hand on my chest. You can feel the pounding of my heart, still hammering away from the intensity of your orgasm, and your lips curl into a smile. I look into your eyes to see a pool of tears resting there until I whisper, "I love you." The tears spill forth and make tiny rivers down your cheeks, and with fingers still trembling, I reach to collect one and bring it to my lips.

Ali Spooner

Tasting the tears of joy, I know I have sampled a little bit of heaven.

Three for the Show

Simone closed the door and locked it behind them when they entered the suite. Del had taken Petra's glass, set it on the table next to the king-sized bed, and was deeply kissing her while her hands were pulling the blouse off Petra's torso. Del broke the kiss long enough to pull the blouse over Petra's head and then resumed the kiss while her hands went to work on Petra's bra. She unfastened the clasps and lowered the straps from Petra's shoulders and then she allowed the bra to fall freely to the floor. Petra slid the short skirt down her hips to join the growing pile of clothes on the floor.

Simone circled their bodies, watching Del's hands engulf Petra's full breasts and begin to knead them while their kiss continued. Simone took a drink from her glass and placed a large ice cube in her mouth while she approached the two women. She leaned down slightly to take Petra's right breast in her mouth, covering the swollen nipple with the ice cube, causing Petra to groan deeply into Del's mouth.

Del broke the kiss and reached around Petra to take an ice cube from Simone's glass, placed it in her mouth, and then she took Petra's left breast into her mouth. Her left hand moved down Petra's body and teased the soft mound of curls with her fingertips.

Petra was delirious while she enjoyed the sensations of having two mouths on her breasts. Each sucked a breast deeply, the ice rapidly melting against her heated skin. Petra's hands worked Simone's shorts off her and she had begun teasing Simone's clit while Del's fingers slipped inside Petra to test her wetness. Petra was soaked with silky moisture and she groaned when she felt Del's fingers slip deep into her entrance.

"Oh yes," Petra moaned, when Del entered her.

Petra lifted her damp fingers to her mouth and her tongue licked Simone's juices from them. "You taste so sweet," she purred to Simone.

"Why don't we take this party to the bed, ladies?" Del suggested.

She watched Simone and Petra laying side by side on the bed, tongues teasing one another while Petra's hand caressed Simone. Del stood at the end of the bed watching while she slowly undressed and then walked into the bathroom to secure the harness around her hips. When she returned to the bedroom, Simone and Petra were still kissing passionately as Petra's fingers stroked deeply inside Simone.

Del crawled onto the bed behind Petra and slipped the tip of the dildo between her soaked lips while Petra and Simone continued to kiss. Del slowly worked the dildo deep inside Petra, matching the rhythm of Petra's fingers sliding in and out of Simone.

Simone's inner muscles clutched at Petra's fingers, while her climax built and Petra thrust faster and harder into her.

Petra was rewarded by Del who also picked up the speed and force of her thrusts while she fucked her hard, rocking their bodies on the bed.

Petra was the first to come and she broke the kiss and screamed to Del that she was coming while her fingers plunged wildly into Simone sending her over the edge to sexual oblivion as well.

Del withdrew from Petra and pulled Simone's hips toward the edge of the bed. She positioned Petra in a kneeling position above Simone's head, facing her. Del leaned in to kiss Petra when Simone's fingers slipped into the moisture between Petra's thighs. Petra was still trembling from her orgasm while Simone glided in and out of her wetness. Del's hands covered Petra's breasts and kneaded them, twisting and tugging at her nipples while she kissed Petra passionately.

Simone reached down, took the dildo in her hand, guiding it between her swollen lips. Del began making slow teasing strokes into her while she pressed Petra's hips lower, moving them closer to Simone's face. Simone withdrew her fingers and replaced them with her tongue buried within Petra while she made deep thrusts inside Petra, drinking in her juices.

Del used Petra's hands to hold Simone's legs wide when she picked up the speed and force of her thrusts. Petra's tongue was dancing wildly in Del's mouth while Simone licked and probed deeply inside her.

Simone covered Petra's clit with her lips. Her fingers plunged back into Petra while she rapidly sucked her clit in and out of her mouth. Petra exploded with pleasure filling Simone's hand and face with her juices.

Del felt Petra's excitement when her orgasm arrived and she drove her hips faster into Simone, thrusting deep while her palm ground harshly across her clit. Simone cried out in rapture when she released her climax and her hips thrashed wildly beneath Del.

Petra released Simone's thighs and then she bent her head down between Simone's legs. Del withdrew and walked across the room to take a sip of her drink and watched Petra's tongue lick along Simone's lips, lapping up the sweet nectar spilling from Simone. Petra remained straddled across Simone's face while the tip of Simone's tongue flicked across her swollen clit. Del listened to the groans and moans of pleasure coming from the two women. She drained her glass then climbed on the bed behind Petra.

Simone felt the shift of weight on the bed when Del arrived and opened her eyes to watch Del slide the dildo inside Petra. She reached between Del's legs to find her soaked and slipped two fingers deep inside her.

Del growled her pleasure while Simone's fingers stroked in at out of her, the intensity of her strokes increased by the thrusts of Del's hips when she fucked Petra.

Simone could feel the muscles inside Del pulsing around her fingers while her thumb located her clit and Del shuddered with pleasure, lunging deeply into Petra until she cried out with pleasure. Petra's moans were muffled, deep inside Simone's body, and the vibration sent Simone tumbling over the edge.

Del withdrew from Petra and relaxed on the bed while all three women gasped to catch their breath. Petra moved carefully from on top of Simone and lay beside Del, her hand toying with Del's nipple.

Simone was facing the opposite direction and watched Petra's fingers tease Del's nipple. Simone still hungered for more from Del and she moved on the bed to straddle Del's waist. Her moan filled the room when the dildo disappeared inside her lust-filled body. Petra watched Simone impale herself onto the dildo, and then leaned over to take Del's right breast deep in her mouth, sucking it vigorously while Simone rode her wildly.

"That looks like it feels so good," Petra cooed to Simone, when her teeth grazed Del's nipple.

Simone opened her eyes and smiled at Petra. "You should try it next," she encouraged her with a wild look in her eyes.

"I think I just might." Petra resumed suckling Del's breast.

Del placed her hand in Petra's hair and lifted her head. "Sit on my face," she instructed.

Petra eagerly moved her hips to straddle Del's face while she leaned forward to engage Simone in a hot kiss. Del slid her hard tongue deep into Petra, then the two women rode Del's body wildly until their arousal peaked and they came together on top of Del.

Simone and Petra exchanged places. Simone smiled at Petra who grinned with pleasure while Del guided the dildo into her and then she slowly lowered her hips.

"Oh my god," Petra cried when she took the full length of the dildo deep into her. "That's so deep and feels so good," she groaned while she ground her hips onto Del.

"Ride it, baby." Del then slipped her tongue into Simone while her fingers twisted Simone's hard nipples.

"Yes, Del," Simone crooned while she watched Petra's eyes cloud over with arousal, her body moving up and down on Del's hips.

Simone had never used a strap on, but she fully intended to change that very soon while she watched the pleasure Petra was receiving. "Faster baby, ride her hard," Simone urged Petra when she heard her gasping for breath.

Sensing Petra was getting close; Del began thrusting her hips to meet Petra's while she plunged down on the dildo.

Petra howled with pleasure and Simone flooded Del's face with a rush of juice when her climax overtook her.

Petra slowly lifted her quivering body off the dildo and rolled onto the bed next to Del.

Simone leaned down to unfasten the harness from Del's waist. Del lifted her hips to allow Simone to remove it and watched with a smile when Simone stepped into the harness and tightened the strap around her waist while she locked eyes with Petra.

"I have got to fuck you," Simone said to Petra.

"Oh yes, Simone," Petra purred. She moved forward to bury her face between Del's spread legs and raised her onto her knees.

Simone walked around to the end of the bed to stand behind Petra. Her hand softly caressed Petra's smooth round ass while Petra lowered her face to Del's mound.

"Fuck me good, Simone," Petra urged, then her tongue flicked out to lightly stroke Del's swollen lips.

"I plan to do just that," Simone promised when her fingers parted Petra's lips and she guided the tip of the dildo to her entrance.

Simone locked eyes with Del. Del could see a feral look in Simone's eyes while she slowly moved her hips forward and the dildo penetrated Petra. The straps of the harness pressed against Simone's lips and she groaned loudly at the pleasure each movement gave her.

"That's it, work it, Simone," Del urged, while Petra's tongue slid into Del's body mimicking the dildo sliding into her wetness.

Del's fingers rubbed her nipples that were aching for attention. Her actions added to the pleasure of Petra's tongue deep inside her vagina.

Watching Del play with her nipples and feeling the movement of Petra's body while she tongue-fucked Del was an incredible turn on for Simone, and it took every ounce of restraint Simone could muster to prevent her from pounding wildly into Petra.

"That feels so good, Petra," Del moaned, while she slowly rolled her hips into her face.

Del noticed how her voice affected Simone's movements and she continued to encourage Petra.

"I want your hot tongue deep inside me, baby, oh yes, that's it," Del purred, while she watched Simone's face.

Simone's hips moved faster until they began to slam into Petra's ass. "Oh yes, faster, Petra, faster baby," Del cried out, while the force of Simone's thrusts pressed Petra's tongue deep inside Del.

Del could feel her orgasm rising in her when Petra breathlessly thrust her tongue deep with each of Simone's thrusts and Simone was grunting from the exertion to her body. "Oh yes, that's it, Petra," Del groaned until she flooded Petra's face with a rush of juices.

Petra removed her tongue and gasped for breath while Simone pounded into her hips. "Yes, yes, yes," she wailed, her body shaking violently while Simone dropped to her knees on the floor completely exhausted.

When Simone could stand, she climbed onto the bed and lay on her back as her muscles trembled uncontrollably from her extreme exertion.

Petra draped herself over Del while her soaked body tingled with pleasure.

Del looked at both women and smiled, content they were both sated, at least for the moment. She rested her head on a pillow and closed her eyes.

†

Del woke to the gentle rocking of the bed. When she opened her eyes, Simone was fucking Petra from behind. She leaned back against the headboard and watched Simone thrust deeply into Petra while she begged for more. Del watched a bead of sweat roll down Simone's breasts and she knew Simone could not keep up the frantic pace for much longer.

Del climbed from the bed, walked into the bathroom, and opened a drawer. Simone had purchased a larger dildo that was still in the package and Del reckoned it was ready to be broken in. She removed the wrapper and rinsed the dildo before she coated its shaft generously with lube. Then she walked behind Simone, who was breathing hard, and whispered. "Let me take over here and you can put Petra's tongue to work."

Simone stopped her motion, slipped out of the harness, then moved in front of Petra and opened her legs wide. Del stepped into the harness and tightened the straps before she removed the dildo from the mount. She handed Petra the dildo. Petra grinned at Simone when she entered her and then lowered her head to softly lick Simone's clit.

Simone had not seen the larger dildo in Del's hand and she smiled when she saw Del slide it down onto the mount. "Oh yes, Del, that is going to feel so good," she urged while Del moved between Petra's legs.

Del placed the head of the dildo between Petra's soaked lips and pushed gently inside. Petra groaned when the larger dildo stretched her lips while Del's hands softly caressed the smooth curves of her ass.

"Relax and I will take you slowly."

Del could feel Petra relax and the dildo moved a little deeper into her. Del gently withdrew and then pushed back in slowly while her hands kneaded Petra's ass. "That's it baby, relax and I'll make it feel so good."

Petra focused her concentration on fucking Simone with the dildo while Del continued to work deeper into her. Petra's body was so very tight, her muscles grasping at the dildo, so that each withdrawal stroke pulled heavily on the harness straps, giving Del great pleasure.

"Feels good, Petra," Simone growled when Petra thrust deeper and faster into Simone. "Oh yes, that's it, fuck me, Petra," Simone begged, while she took the full length of the dildo deep inside her. Simone quivered when Petra's mouth covered her clit and ground her teeth against her; until Simone cried out, she was coming.

Petra gasped for air while she rested her cheek against Simone's stomach. Simone stroked through her hair while Del continued to drive the dildo deeper into Petra.

"Relax baby and take it," Simone whispered.

"It's so big," Petra moaned, when Del filled her completely.

When the dildo's length buried inside Petra, Del stopped her movement. She leaned over her and whispered into her ear, "There, that's it and you have taken it all."

Del's hand circled Petra's body and her finger found her clit engorged with blood. She softly stroked across her clit while Petra closed her eyes attempting to hold back her pleasure.

"Doesn't that feel good?" Del asked.

"Oh yes, Del," Petra whispered.

"Are you ready for more?"

"Fuck me, Del," Petra groaned.

Simone smiled at Del who was pleased that Petra had turned out to be such a lusty lover. Not to miss this pleasuring, Simone turned and scooted her body under Petra then took her clit in her mouth.

Del took Petra's hips in her hands, holding them in place while she rocked slowly back and forth making short strokes and Petra adjusted to the new dildo. Del could feel Petra begin to enjoy the dildo when her body secreted extra lubricant to coat her walls allowing Del to move more fluidly inside her.

Simone still had the dildo buried inside her and Petra began to stroke her with the same rhythm Del was moving into her. Simone began to writhe on the bed beneath Petra, her body eager for Del to fuck her. She prayed Petra would come soon, so she could have Del buried deep inside her.

Del stroked smoothly into Petra, slowly building up speed while Petra's moans grew louder and mixed with Simone's when they both approached their climax. Simone convulsed with pleasure when Petra buried the dildo inside her and rubbed her clit roughly with her palm.

Petra could no longer hold back her climax. Her body flooded Simone's face while she shook violently with intense pleasure and she collapsed on top of Simone.

Del carefully withdrew from Petra and rested on the bed.

Simone eagerly awaited Del's attention and when Del had left her screaming with pleasure, the three of them collapsed onto sweaty tangled sheets and slept well into the afternoon.

†

Movement on the bed woke Simone as Petra carefully climbed from the bed. "I'm going to go to my room, but I'll see you two later, if that's okay?"

"That's perfect," she answered. "Last night was fantastic and I hope we can have a repeat performance tonight."

"I'd like that," Petra answered as she slipped back into her clothing. She returned to the bed to kiss Simone softly. "Later, lover," she whispered and left the room.

†

Simone watched Del sleeping, her naked torso exposed, free of the twisted sheet around her waist. She had to admit Del had been a creative and eager lover who had more than satisfied her desires. Another day or two on the island and she would probably never see Del again, but she planned to make the most of her during the time they spent together. Now that Petra had gone, and it was just the two of them once more, she had a good idea of how they'd spend the afternoon.

She reached across to lightly caress Del's exposed chest, her fingernails brushing across sleeping nipples. Del moaned from the teasing touch and her eyes flew open to watch Simone's hand glide over her skin. She smiled at Simone and opened her arms, inviting her beautiful lover into an embrace.

About the Author

Ali Spooner

Ali Spooner, a native of Florida, calls Pensacola her forever home. Ali has been writing for many years as a hobby, and with the assistance of the Affinity team, she has taken her love of storytelling to a new level. Ali's character's range from cowgirls and psychics to a healthy dose of supernatural beings. She has written stand-alone titles as well as series. Ali is an avid reader and her other hobbies include photography, outdoor activities, and watching college sports.

Other Books from Affinity eBook Press

The Promise by JM Dragon
An accidental meeting with Melissa Grant, leads to an unexpected offer for Kris Lake—refurbishing a beach cottage, with the help of Melissa's granddaughter Claire. Do outer imperfections prevent them from reaching the beauty that lives inside and the chance of a happy new life? Find out in this lovely romance that will fill you with heart-warming sensations throughout the story.

Christmas at Winterbourne by Jen Silver
The Christmas festivities for the guests booked into Winterbourne House has all the goings-on of a traditional holiday. The only difference is that this guesthouse is run by lesbians, for lesbians. Join the guests and staff at Winterbourne for a Christmas you'll not soon forget.

The Review by Annette Mori
Silver Lining, a successful lesbian romance writer, has the crazy idea to sponsor a contest where the first reader who posts a review wins a home-cooked meal with an offer to fly

the winner to Washington State. Jasmine, the winner, has engaged in subtle flirtations with Silver. Bizarre messages from the unknown fan has Silver questioning the wisdom of a relationship with Jasmine.

South of Heaven by Ali Spooner
Kendra Drake has taken over as Captain of her father's shrimp boat. As a favor to her father, Kendra has agreed to give fellow shrimper, Lindsey Bowen, a chance to work on the boat but first must prove herself to Kendra and her crew. Lindsey finds a way into Kendra's heart. Will it only last for the summer?

Catch to Release by Lacey Schmidt
On the verge of success, lesbian folk-rock star, Shay Greenaura, finds herself caught up in more than just her music. Threats have her manager hiring a security firm for protection. Addison Weller, a former Diplomatic Security Services agent is called in to assess the threats against Shay. Their undeniable attraction, brewing silently between them, could prove to be a fatal distraction. Follow this fast-paced adventure to its surprising romantic conclusion.

Ready for Love by Erin O'Reilly
Kylie Wilcox's life dramatically changed with the death of her husband. Dr. LJ Evans, a renowned archaeologist, needed and wanted nothing but her work for her happiness. Their worlds are about to collide and lives will be altered forever.

Neptune's Ring by Ali Spooner
In the sequel to *Venus Rising*, Nat and Liz, owners of Venus Rising, invite Levi and Vanessa to join them in a venture for

a new club on another island. They find the perfect place in an unfinished resort, Neptune's Ring. While on the island, Levi is drawn into a mystery involving secret compartments and a murder. Join the characters in this page-turning adventure, filled with steamy romance, intrigue, and an unsolved murder.

The Ultimate Betrayal by Annette Mori
Lara is a successful, beautiful, charming, financier. She is also a total control freak, so whatever Lara wants, Lara makes sure she gets. Rachel is Lara's fun-loving, charming, irresistible wife. Sophia's surprise visit to see Lara sets in motion a number of life changing events for them all. Hell has no fury as a woman scorned.

It's in Her Kiss by Various Affinity Authors
A collection of various holiday stories dedicated to anyone and everyone that reads it. Young, old, lesbian, gay, bisexual, and transgender. We are all the same inside and want the same things outside...love, happiness, and that special someone to spend all of our holidays with.

Keeping Faith by TJ Vertigo
You loved them in the previous novels, Private Dancer, Reece's Faith, and Reece's Star, now join the antics of Reece, Faith, Cori, Vi, and even The Animal, one last time in *Keeping Faith*.

Bound by Ali Spooner
A rogue, master vampire threatens the existence of the New Orleans vampire clan. Lord Jordan enlists Devin Benoit,

sister of the Baton Rouge Alpha, and her witch lover, Tia, to assist with cleansing the city from potential disaster.

The Circle Dance by Jen Silver
Jamie Steele has moved to another town, trying to forget the heartbreak of losing her lover of six years. Sasha Fairfield finds her thoughts taken up with her ex-lover and thinks she wants Jamie back. Follow this captivating romance as love dances through the lives of these women to its surprising conclusion.

Search for the White Moon by Natalie London
Kathryn Austin, a government agent, is given opera singer Adriana Desi as her new assignment. Their lives and futures are in danger as the White Moon terrorists hunt them. Immerse yourself in this fast-paced, romantic thriller by debut author Natalie London.

Take Me as I Am by JM Dragon & Erin O'Reilly
When Jo Lackerly and Thea Danvers meet, an unexpected friendship develops, proving a catalyst for both women to change their lives irrevocably. Follow them on a journey of discovery that will have your heart smiling, blood boiling, and senses entangled in a wonderful romance.

Carved in Stone by Jen Silver
Join the characters from *Starting Over* and *Arc Over Time* in this final book from the Starling Hill trilogy. Ellie Winters thinks she might be going mad when the ancient queen wants a proper burial for herself and her consort. *Carved in Stone* has romance, adventure, a treasure hunt, and happy endings for all, living and dead.

Anywhere, Everywhere by Renee MacKenzie
Gwen Martin's life in the Ten Thousand Islands area changes irrevocably when Piper Jackson comes into her life. Without trust, can the budding relationship between Gwen and Piper survive? Or will the answers to the questions continue to haunt them?

Venus Rising by Ali Spooner
Levi Johnson arrives at Venus Rising, an exclusive, lesbian-only tropical resort in the Virgin Islands, and finds more than she expected—a sizzling-hot love triangle. Torn between her attraction to both women, Levi struggles to choose the right woman to share her life.

The Devil's Tree by Ali Spooner
Torn between her love for the pack and her need to find what's missing in her life, Devin Benoit travels to New Orleans. Will the previous happenings at the Devil's Tree help or hinder Devin in the fight for her life, and the life of Tia, the woman who now owns her heart?

The Beggars' Coppice by Erica Lawson
Edda Case is a woman in crisis who discovers that things are not as they seem. Is it truly a message for her from beyond the grave, or is something more sinister taking place? Can Edda solve the mystery of *The Beggars' Coppice*?

E-Books, Print, Free e-books

Visit our website for more publications available online.

www.affinityebooks.com

Published by Affinity E-Book Press NZ LTD
Canterbury, New Zealand

Registered Company 2517228

www.ingramcontent.com/pod-product-compliance
Lightning Source LLC
Chambersburg PA
CBHW070106260626
47160CB00004B/1344